A DEADLY PLAN REVEALED

"You have information that something is wrong in the South, in the West?"

"Let me say I had grounds for suspicion," Miss Majoribanks replied. "And then this letter from my brother. When I received it, I acted at once. I got out the ledgers and read all the information we had on the Louisiana Territory, read the reports of Lewis and Clark and the letters from James Mackay. What my brother has discovered, Mr. Tate, is a plot to seize the Louisiana Territory and to make an independent kingdom of it."

"That's nonsense."

She shrugged. "Exactly the reaction from our senator, Mr. Tate. I approached him on the matter. He either does not believe anything I say or has reasons for not wishing to believe."

"Miss Majoribanks, you must remember, you are a very young lady."

"Mr. Tate, I have told you all this not only to give you my reasons for going west, but because I hope you will see the necessity for prompt action."

"The man who is to direct the subversive movements in the Louisiana Territory may already be en route. I know much of this man. He is a devil incarnate, who will stop at nothing. . . ."

Bantam Books by Louis L'Amour

NOVELS

Bendigo Shafter
Borden Chantry
Brionne
The Broken Gun
The Burning Hills
The Californios
Callaghen
Catlow
Chancy
The Cherokee Trail
Comstock Lode
Conagher
Crossfire Trail
Dark Canyon
Down the Long Hills
The Empty Land
Fair Blows the Wind
Fallon
The Ferguson Rifle
The First Fast Draw
Flint
Guns of the Timberlands
Hanging Woman Creek
The Haunted Mesa
Heller with a Gun
The High Graders
High Lonesome
Hondo
How the West Was Won
The Iron Marshal
The Key-Lock Man
Kid Rodelo
Kilkenny
Killoe
Kilrone
Kiowa Trail
Last of the Breed
Last Stand at Papago Wells
The Lonesome Gods
The Man Called Noon
The Man from Skibbereen
The Man from the Broken Hills
Matagorda
Milo Talon
The Mountain Valley War
North to the Rails
Over on the Dry Side
Passin' Through
The Proving Trail
The Quick and the Dead
Radigan
Reilly's Luck
The Rider of Lost Creek
Rivers West
The Shadow Riders
Shalako
Showdown at Yellow Butte
Silver Canyon
Sitka
Son of a Wanted Man
Taggart
The Tall Stranger
To Tame a Land
Tucker
Under the Sweetwater Rim
Utah Blaine
The Walking Drum
Westward the Tide
Where the Long Grass Blows

SHORT STORY COLLECTIONS

Beyond the Great Snow Mountains
Bowdrie
Bowdrie's Law
Buckskin Run
The Collected Short Stories of Louis L'Amour (vols. 1–7)
Dutchman's Flat
End of the Drive
From the Listening Hills
The Hills of Homicide
Law of the Desert Born
Long Ride Home
Lonigan
May There Be a Road
Monument Rock
Night Over the Solomons
Off the Mangrove Coast
The Outlaws of Mesquite
The Rider of the Ruby Hills
Riding for the Brand
The Strong Shall Live
The Trail to Crazy Man
Valley of the Sun
War Party
West from Singapore
West of Dodge
With These Hands
Yondering

SACKETT TITLES

Sackett's Land
To the Far Blue Mountains
The Warrior's Path
Jubal Sackett
Ride the River
The Daybreakers
Sackett
Lando
Mojave Crossing
Mustang Man
The Lonely Men
Galloway
Treasure Mountain
Lonely on the Mountain
Ride the Dark Trail
The Sackett Brand
The Sky-Liners

THE HOPALONG CASSIDY NOVELS

The Riders of High Rock
The Rustlers of West Fork
The Trail to Seven Pines
Trouble Shooter

NONFICTION

Education of a Wandering Man
Frontier
The Sackett Companion: A Personal Guide to the Sackett Novels
A Trail of Memories: The Quotations of Louis L'Amour, compiled by Angelique L'Amour

POETRY

Smoke from This Altar

LOST TREASURES

Louis L'Amour's Lost Treasures: Volume 1 (with Beau L'Amour)
No Traveller Returns (with Beau L'Amour)
Louis L'Amour's Lost Treasures: Volume 2 (with Beau L'Amour)

RIVERS WEST

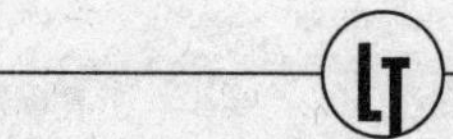

A NOVEL

Louis L'Amour

BANTAM
NEW YORK

Bantam Books
An imprint of Random House
A division of Penguin Random House LLC
1745 Broadway, New York, NY 10019
randomhousebooks.com
penguinrandomhouse.com

2025 Bantam Books Mass Market Edition

Originally published in the United States
by Bantam Books, an imprint of Random House, a division of
Penguin Random House LLC, in 1975.

ISBN 978-0-593-35557-2
Ebook ISBN 978-0-553-89968-9

Cover art: Gordon Crabb

Photograph of Louis L'Amour:
John Hamilton—Globe Photos, Inc.

Printed in the United States of America

2 4 6 8 9 7 5 3 1

Bantam Books mass market edition: October 2025

Book design by Edwin A. Vazquez

The authorized representative in the EU for product safety and compliance is Penguin Random House Ireland,
Morrison Chambers, 32 Nassau Street,
Dublin D02 YH68, Ireland.
https://eu-contact.penguin.ie

RIVERS WEST

THE UNITED STATES
AND THE
LOUISIANA PURCHASE
1821
Scale of Miles
0
100
200
300
400
BLACKFOOT
Lake of the Woods
49th Parallel
Rainy Lake
Lake Superior
MICHIGAN
TERR.
CROW
LOUISIANA
PURCHASE
Lake Michigan
Fort Armstrong
42nd Parallel
Fort Atkinson
INDIANA
Platte R.
SIOUX
ILLINOIS
ROCKY MTS.
Bonhomme Island
Kansas R.
Cold Water Creek
Missouri R.
MISSOURI TERRITORY
St. Louis
Ohio R.
Mississippi R.
TENNESSEE
Santa Fe
Arkansas R.
ARKANSAS TERRITORY
MISSISSIPPI
ALAB.
LOUISIANA
Natchez
SPANISH TERRITORY

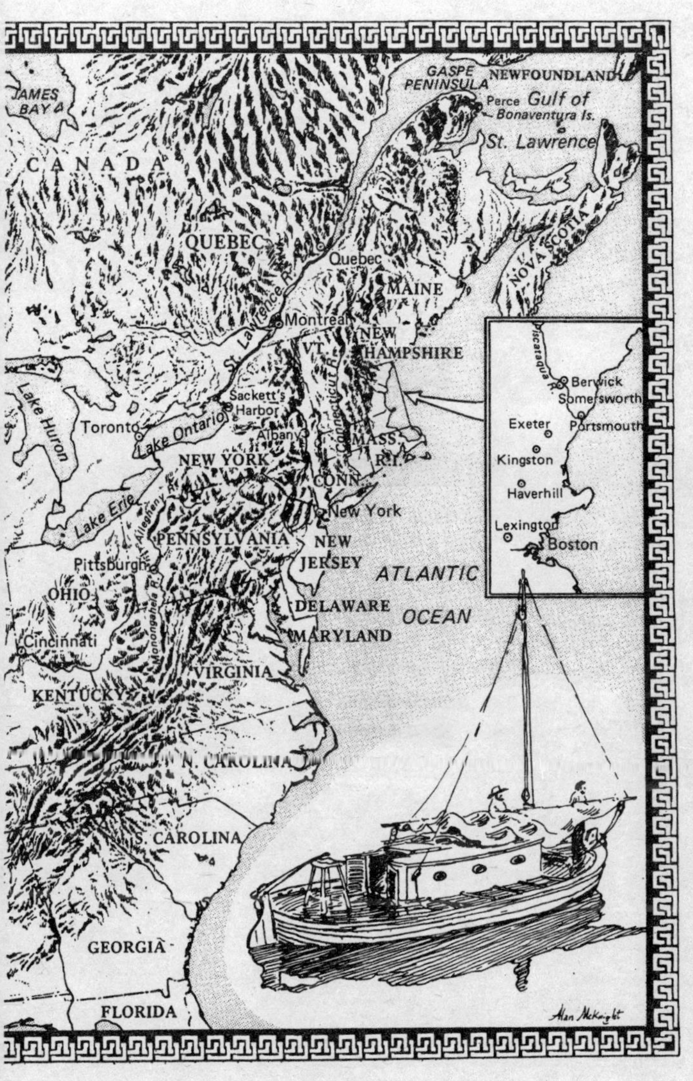
JAMES BAY
CANADA
GASPE PENINSULA
NEWFOUNDLAND
Perce
Gulf of
Bonaventura Is.
St. Lawrence
QUEBEC
Quebec
NOVA SCOTIA
MAINE
St. Lawrence R.
Montreal
VT.
NEW HAMPSHIRE
Connecticut R.
Piscataqua R.
Berwick
Somersworth
Portsmouth
Exeter
Kingston
Haverhill
Lexington
Boston
Lake Huron
Sackett's Harbor
Toronto
Lake Ontario
Albany
MASS.
R.I.
NEW YORK
CONN.
Lake Erie
Allegheny R.
New York
PENNSYLVANIA
NEW JERSEY
ATLANTIC
OCEAN
Pittsburgh
OHIO
Monongahela R.
DELAWARE
MARYLAND
Cincinnati
VIRGINIA
KENTUCKY
N. CAROLINA
S. CAROLINA
GEORGIA
FLORIDA
Alan McKnight

CHAPTER I

A GHOST TRAIL, A DARK TRAIL, a trail endlessly winding. A dark cavern under enormous trees down which blew a cold wind that skimmed the pools with ice. A corduroy road made from logs laid side by side, logs slippery with mud and slush, with rotting vegetation from the swamp.

Here and there a log had sunk deep, leaving a cleft into which a suddenly plunged foot could mean a broken leg, and on either side the swamp . . . some said it was bottomless. Horses had sunk out there, never to be seen again, and men, also.

My father's house lay several days behind me, back of a shoulder of the Quebec shore above the Gulf of St. Lawrence. For days I had been walking southward. An owl glided past with a measured beat of great, slow wings, and out in the swamp some unseen creature moved.

Was that a step behind me?

Astride a gap between logs, I paused to listen, half-turned to look.

Nothing . . . I must have been mistaken. Yet, I had heard *something*.

My shoulders ached from the burden of my tools. Soon I would have to purchase a mule, a horse or an ox. For the tools I must have with me. Of what use is a shipwright without tools?

Straining my eyes in the darkness I looked for a place to stop, any place in which to rest, if ever so briefly. And then I saw a wide stump from which a tree had been sawed, a full six feet in diameter . . . and the tree cut from it lay in the swamp close by, half-sunk.

With my left hand I swung the tools to the stump, keeping the rifle in my right, ready for use. This was a far, wild place. There were few travellers and fewer still were honest men. Young I might be, but not trusting.

For the first time I was leaving home, going south from Canada into the United States. Westward, it was said, they were building, and we are builders, we Talons.

There was a time when at least one of the family had been a pirate, a fierce old man even in his later years, I'd been told. He had sailed the far waters of the Indian Ocean, the Bay of Bengal, and the Red Sea, but mostly off the Coromandel and Malabar coasts of India. He'd done well, too, or so it was said. I'd seen none of the treasure he was said to have brought away. Not a man who worked in timber or stone, but even he had been an artist of sorts, a fine hand at carving and metal work even as a child.

What was *that*? I half-rose from my seat on the stump, then settled back, holding my rifle in both hands.

It was cold, and growing colder.

Behind me, on the Gaspe, I had left only my father's cottage and the good will of a few of my neighbors. My father was gone. My mother had died when I was yet a young boy, and I had no sweetheart.

Of course, there had been a girl. We had roamed the fields together as children, danced together, even talked of marriage. That was before a man far wealthier than I had come to see her father. To be wealthier than I was not difficult, for I had only the cottage inherited from my father, along with my trade, and she was ambitious.

The other man was a merchant with many acres, a three-masted schooner trading along the coast, and a store. He was a landed and moneyed man and, as I have said, she was ambitious.

She had come to our meeting place one last time, and immediately I could tell something was different. There was to be no fooling about on this day, for she was very serious. "Jean," she pronounced it *Zhan* as was correct, but with an inflection that was her own, "my father wants me to marry Henry Barboure."

It took a moment for me to understand. Barboure was nearly forty, twice as old as I, and a respected, successful man, although I'd heard it said he was close-fisted and a hard one with whom to deal.

"You are not going to?" I protested.

"I must, unless . . . unless . . . ?"

"Unless what?"

"Jean, do you know where the treasure is? I mean all that gold the old man left. He was your great-grandfather, wasn't he? The pirate?"

"It was further back than that," I said, "and anyway, he left no gold. None that I know of."

She came closer to me. "I *know* it is a family secret. But Jean . . . if we had all that gold . . . well, father would never think of asking me to marry Henry. He always told me that you knew where it was, and you could get it . . . some of it . . . whenever you liked."

So that was it. The gold. Of course, I knew the stories, for they had been legend in the Gaspe since the old man's time. He had been one of the first to settle on what was then a lonely, almost uninhabited coast. He had built a strong stone castle . . . burned by the British during one of their raids many years after, and attacked many times before that.

The story was that he had hidden a great treasure, that he could dip into it whenever he wished. He had bought property, a good deal of it. And it was true he had sailed to Quebec City or Montreal . . . even down to Boston or New York to buy whatever he wished. But I knew nothing of any treasure, nothing at all.

My father had shrugged off the stories. "Nonsense!" he would say. "Think nothing of treasure or stories of treasure. You will have in this world only what you earn . . . and save. Remember that. Do not waste your life in a vain search for a treasure that may not exist."

"There is no treasure," I said to her. "It is all a silly story."

"But he had money!" she protested. "He was fabulously rich!"

"And he spent it," I said. "If you want me it shall be as I am, a man with a good trade, who can make a good living."

She was scornful. "A good living! Do you think that is all I want? Henry can give me everything! A beautiful home, travel, money to spend, beautiful clothes . . . !"

"Take him then," I had told her. "Take him, and be damned!"

Perhaps I spoke too harshly. She left me then, and the next time we met on the street she walked by me as if I had not existed.

My heart, I told myself, was broken. For a week I tried

to convince myself of it. I tried to write poetry about it, I told myself my life was ruined and had a great time playing with the drama of it, but not for a minute was I really fooled. Actually, only my vanity had suffered, and that not very much. In fact, I was relieved. Now I was free to go out into the world.

Had not we Talons always done so? Talons, that is, of my blood. Others might have the same name, but we of our family knew from whence it came, and how our pirate ancestor had his hand chopped off by a tyrant, and had fashioned an ingenious metal claw to replace it. From that he had taken the name we bore. Talon.

When I was a boy there was an old man in the village who claimed that, when he was a child, he had known the first Talon. He never mentioned the name without a quick glance over the shoulder. Perhaps our family had taken to the building trades and worked to be known as solid and reliable craftsmen in order to put that reputation behind us. It made for a romantic story but it did not confer trust. Good or bad I had my own name to make.

A splash of water . . . a stir from the swamp.

The muzzle of my rifle shifted to cover the spot. It was an eerie place this, and I should be on my way.

Suddenly my throat choked with fear. From the dark, oily waters of the swamp, a white hand lifted . . . lifted, faint, ghost-like . . . it seemed to beckon.

I was on my feet, thumb on the hammer; ready to rear back and fire.

Then slowly the hand became an arm. It dropped over a log, and then a head lifted from the water, a strained white face, gasping . . . pleading . . . reaching out.

I sprang forward and caught at the hand.

It was cold . . . cold. But it was the hand of no ghost. It was flesh and bone. I hauled upon the arm and a body emerged from the swamp and fell across the half-submerged log. Gently then, I turned him over.

"Help," the voice was faint, "help me, I—"

There was a stab wound in his chest, a deep wound from which blood and water bubbled. The man was dying. Had I anything with which to treat him, his life still could not be saved.

"—stabbed me. He knew who I was, he—" the voice faded.

"Easy, now!" I warned. I loosened his collar, then tried to ease his position. I'd no idea what he was talking about, nor what to do. He was badly hurt, but from the appearance of the wound I feared the knife had penetrated a lung.

There was another stab wound in his side, and there might be others in his back. We were in the midst of a swamp, on a makeshift corduroy log road that was almost half under water and there was no dry land anywhere about that I could see. Nor any place to build a fire. To carry the man in this condition was unthinkable.

"Sir," I said, "there's not much I can do."

He turned his eyes on me and seemed conscious of me for the first time. "I know," he said, his voice suddenly quiet, "and I'd rather you . . . you didn't try. I'm . . . I'm somewhat comfortable.

"Got me in the back. He . . . he got me three times before I was able to turn around. I don't believe I . . . I even scratched . . . him.

"A bad man . . . stop at nothing . . . at nothing at all."

He caught my hand. "I am Captain Rob . . . Robert Foulsham."

"American?"

"British."

It was damp and gloomy. I was far from where I wished to be, which was an inn, somewhere in the five miles that lay before me. It was already late.

He muttered, talked lucidly, then wandered. I stayed close beside him, wishing there was something I could do. He was far gone, and growing weaker.

"Get him!" he spoke suddenly, loudly. "He is . . . a traitor. He will destroy . . . destroy. He is—" His voice wandered off and he was silent.

"Who was it killed you?" I asked. Then, realizing how my words must sound, I said, "Who attacked you?"

"Torville . . . Baron Richard Torville."

"What's he like? Is he tall? Is he—?"

It was no use, for the man had died.

I got slowly to my feet and stood looking down at him. What could I do? What should I do? I had no heart to sink him in the swamp, and there was no way to bury him. Yet to leave him where he lay seemed a shameful thing.

If he had relatives, they—

Relatives! I knelt beside the body and went carefully through his pockets. There were some soaked and stained papers, yet there were others in a sealed leather packet. I went carefully through the pockets, found several gold pieces, and in a belt about the waist, several more.

There was a pistol, useless until dried out and recharged. A small pistol it was, though very admirably made.

The few things I gathered together. When I reached a city I would try to mail them . . . for among the things there might be the address of his relatives or acquaintances.

He was young . . . older than I but less than thirty, and quite fit. From his youth I decided the title of captain was rather military than maritime.

I had straightened from my final task when I heard a faint splash . . . a stir or something, of movement. My rifle came waist high, held easily in my hands.

The sounds came nearer, a step and a swish, a hit and a miss.

Who could be on the road on such a night? Certainly, I had been a fool to attempt to reach my destination before night fell, and the captain here had been, apparently, pursuing someone. Suddenly a figure loomed in the darkness.

"Come along," I said, "if you're friendly, come easy with your hands in sight. If you're not friendly I can split you right up the middle."

"Avast there! Avast, lad. I'm coming in peaceful, wishing no harm to any man or beast . . . least of all, to me."

He was six or seven inches taller than my five feet and ten inches, with shoulders like a yard-arm, and he had a peg-leg. He also wore a black beard and there was a gold ring in at least one ear.

Armed, too. I could see he carried both a rifle and a dirk.

"You travel late," I said.

He glanced down at the body. "Did you kill him?" His eyes gleamed at me.

"I did not . . . did you?" For certainly he looked the murderer if ever a man did.

"Not I." He peered at the body. "Well, well. A fine handsome young chap to die so easily. I've killed a few in my time, but not that one." He grinned at me. "Anyway, I've just come up. You stand over the body and that man is freshly dead. The law will ask questions, so you'd better think of some answers."

"There is no law here," I said. "This is the forest. Yet it is no way for a man to die."

The big man shrugged. "Who is to say where a man should die? He dies when his time comes, no matter where." Then, a might wistfully, he added, "Only the body of the man is here. What was inside him is gone. So where he lies does not matter."

He gestured down the way. "I am told there's an inn. Are you for it?"

"I am."

We started on then, leaving the body where it lay for lack of a better thing to do.

The big man wore an old cocked hat and a cloak that made him look even more huge in the darkness. "How far is it, do you suppose? I have come far, and this leg of mine, it does not favor long walks."

"Five miles . . . perhaps less. Sometimes the understanding of miles is not well grasped. Five miles can mean over the hill and around the bend or it can mean all day."

"I know." He peered at me. "You've a load there. Is it tools you carry?"

"Tools of my trade. I am a shipwright."

"In the forest?" He stared at me. "You are to build ships in the forest?"

What my destination was, and why, was none of his business, so I simply said, "South of here are many seaports where they build vessels to trade with the Indies or ships for whaling."

"You've a French sound to your voice."

"I am French . . . in part, but Canadian born, and pleased to be."

We walked on in silence, splashing and slipping, swearing a little and grunting. "I am called Jambe-de-Bois," he said suddenly, "because of this," he indicated the leg.

"It is as good as another," I said, "a name is what a man makes of it."

"True, lad . . . true." He glanced at me. "And you? You have a name?"

Suddenly, I was wary. Who was this man from out of the night, coming upon me standing over a dead man and making little of it? Why this sudden interest in my name? For his tone seemed to have sharpened just a little at the question. Moreover, there was about him something vaguely familiar.

"Who does not have a name? I find them of small meaning."

Five feet ten inches, I was, and shorter than him. He looked to be a powerful man, but I yielded him nothing on that score. For I was big-boned and muscled, in part it was inheritance, for mine had been a strong family, and in part it was my trade and the handling of heavy timbers and my tools. I believed myself the equal of any man when it came to sheer strength.

Who was he? And where was he going? I longed to ask but had scarcely the right, having refused to tell my name. The vague familiarity about him worried me. I was far from home, yet this man had a feel of the sea about him and something of our own accent in his speech. Had he followed me? Was that absurd story of treasure to haunt me forever?

We slopped along in the darkness, wary of our footsteps, only occasionally glimpsing a star overhead through the lace-work of branches. Despite his peg-leg he swung along easily as I, and I fancy myself as a man who can walk.

Then, through the dark columns of the huge old trees, we saw a light. With the chance of food and drink before us, we lengthened our strides, and in a few minutes faced a clearing under giant trees, and a ramshackle bridge over an arm of the swamp.

The latch-string was out, and we lifted it, and stepped inside.

A fine fire blazed upon the hearth of a huge fireplace at the opposite end of the room. There was a long table, some benches, and a half-dozen men standing about. At the fire a thin woman in ill-fitting clothes stirred something in a pot that set my stomach to rumbling.

A bald-headed man with a fringe of sandy hair whom I took to be the owner, looked around at us. He wore a long buckskin waist-coat and heavy boots.

"Welcome, lads! Welcome! Come up to the table! It's a raw night for the out of doors. Have a nip of something. I've rum . . . even a bit of ale that I've brewed m'self. Tasty . . . mighty tasty."

He turned to the woman at the fire. "Bett, get some food on the table. These will be hungry men."

There was a tall man with his back to the wall, a handsome man indeed, with a pipe in one hand and a glass in the other. He took me in with a quick, appraising glance. My coat was open, and he could see the pistol there.

I set my tools in the corner, and after a moment of hesitation, my rifle beside them.

CHAPTER II

"MY NAME IS WATSON," the bald-headed man said. "We do a bit of farming here, and some 'at o' fishing, and a man with a rifle can find game. We set a good table, if'n I do say so m'self."

He glanced from Jambe to me. "A tot of rum? Warms a body who's been out in the cold night."

"Aye," I agreed, "it has been a long way of forest and swamp."

"Here it is! And good Jamaica, too! I've a taste for the dark rum. Nothing fancy, just good rum."

The rum did take the chill from my bones, but it was food I wanted, and besides, I'd no taste for drinking with strangers about, and there was an air in this place I did not like. Watson was all right, no doubt, but by nature I am a cautious man and the look of the others was not to my taste.

There was a dark, sallow man with snaky black eyes. He stared at me. "Goin' far?" he asked.

"As far as a job," I said. "Word has come to me that they are building ships down Boston way."

By saying that I was lying, for my interest lay westward rather than south. To the frontier town of Pittsburgh. Two or three years before they'd built the steamer, *New Orleans,* said to be the first on western waters, and I had a feeling it was to be the first of many. With the fur trade growing to the westward there would be a demand for fast, reliable transportation, and if the *New Orleans* had proved itself, they would build others. I had a dream of building my own boat to trade on the western waters.

The tall man with the pipe moved around the table and dropped to the bench opposite me. His smile was pleasant but the expression in his eyes was calculating; and somehow taunting. I had a feeling that here was a man who looked with amused contempt on all about him.

"Colonel Rodney Macklem," he said, introducing himself. "Will you have a drink?"

"Obliged, but I have a drink."

"You didn't mention your name."

"John Daniel," I said it easily, but there was a flicker of irritation in his eyes, of impatience, too. Here was a man who did not wish to be thwarted or turned aside, yet his lips smiled in a friendly fashion. I had just a thought, however, that he had expected another name . . . what name?

Jambe-de-Bois was watching me, too, somewhat puzzled, no doubt, and curious.

Bett Watson came around the table with a huge bowl of stew and two smaller ones, and with spoons and a ladle. "Start on that," she said cheerfully.

Untidy, but clean, she was a blowsy, red-cheeked woman with a cheerful air. "There's more coming," she added.

Macklem lighted his pipe again. He avoided the eyes of Jambe-de-Bois and Jambe did likewise. Did they know each other? Did they recall something each would prefer forgotten?

The talk in the room was rambling, mostly of trail conditions and weather, for it was these by which we lived. Macklem was casual, talking little. Of the body we had found I decided to say nothing, yet I listened for some word of travellers. One of these men might have seen his killer, one might even be his killer . . . although I doubted that.

The murdered man had been a British army officer, and for some reason he had been pursuing the man who killed him.

Why?

Why the pursuit, and why the killing? This was no simple robbery, although every trail was beset with thieves, and every inn such as this a possible lurking place for them. It was no unusual thing to find a traveller murdered or to have one simply disappear.

The cabin was more than just the one room, but from the outside it had not appeared to be large. No doubt we would sleep on the floor in this room. Watson was even now stoking the fire adding a couple of heavy logs that would hold it through the night.

The stew tasted good, when it was finished Bett Watson brought a big chunk of plum pudding and a pot of coffee.

Aside from Macklem those in the room were a rough-looking crew, yet I suspect I looked equally rough myself.

He said, "You are French?"

"In part."

"You have a familiar look, John Daniel. I think I have seen you before . . . or someone very much like you."

I shrugged. "Perhaps . . . who knows? I have been here and there."

He was not satisfied, and continued to talk, but his comments were leading, his questions insidious. Obviously, he wished very much to know who I was, and he was not satisfied that I was a shipwright. Yet, he was pleasant enough, and an agreeable talker.

The air in the room was close and warm, too warm. I felt sleepy, tired from the hike. Not that I had walked far, for twenty miles was nothing exceptional, but the walking had been rough, the footing uncertain. However, I did not want to sleep. Not until they all did.

I thought of the water-proof envelope inside my shirt, and the water-soaked papers. Finding myself in a reasonably well lit room their contents had my curiosity aroused but I had no idea of examining the papers here. I wanted to answer no questions. The big, good-looking man . . . Macklem . . . had noticed Foulsham's pistol. Was it just because pistols were rarely carried by working-men like myself? Or did he know that particular gun?

Watson and one of the others moved the table aside and we spread our beds on the floor. All of us carried blankets . . . a man couldn't travel without them, and even in the larger taverns a man was often expected to have his own bedding.

Long after the candles were blown out and only the firelight played on the ceiling, I lay awake, considering. That man had been murdered for a reason. He was following the man who had murdered him, and after being stabbed had fallen or been thrown into the swamp. Therefore, the murderer could assume no body had been found, and that he was free from worry.

Two other considerations remained. Either the murderer had searched the body or he had not. If he had searched it, he had not wanted either the gold or the papers or the pistol. If he had not been able to search the body he might still want those papers, if they were of value to him.

It might be that in the struggle the dying man had fallen into the swamp where the killer could not reach him. In any event, it behooved me to be very careful to let no one know I'd seen the dead man or talked to him, or had examined the body. Jambe did know, but had shown no urge to discuss it. Was he the murderer? Might he not have concealed himself when he heard me coming?

Under my blankets I drew my knife sheath off of my belt. My work often called for a knife, and most men carried them as a tool if not as a weapon. Mine was razor-sharp, with a point like a needle. Slipping the sheathed knife between my leg and the floor, I went to sleep with my fingers lightly touching its handle.

The last thing I recalled was firelight flickering on the roof, and the next thing was a dim red glow with a black figure looming above me and my blanket gently drawn back. As another hand reached for the inside of my shirt, I rolled slightly, putting my weight on the scabbard, and drew the blade. Barely thinking, barely awake, I thrust the knife sharply upward. The thief, whoever he was, jerked away and vanished.

Vanished.

I sat up quickly, then came unsteadily to my feet, knife in hand. I blinked away sleep. What had happened? Where had he gone?

All was dark and still. Nothing moved. There was a faint glow from the fire, a reddish glow that flickered on some of the faces, threw others into deeper shadow.

Stepping across the sleeping men I sheathed my blade and taking the poker, stirred the fire, then added some smaller sticks. The fire blazed up, and the room grew lighter.

Six men lay on the floor, all seemed to be sleeping. I looked around the room . . . nothing.

One of the men lying there was faking . . . at least one, and possibly more. One of those men would have robbed, perhaps murdered me.

Which one?

For a moment I looked at them, then went back to my bed and lay down.

It might have been a simple attempt at robbery, but a man never knew. I lay awake, staring up at the roof and listening. Light was breaking before I dozed off again but only for a few minutes and then they were all getting up.

Pulling on my boots I stood up and started to shove the pistol behind my belt.

Macklem extended a hand, "That's an interesting weapon. May I see it?"

I tucked the pistol behind my belt and let my coat fall into place, concealing it. "It is simply a pistol, like any other," I said coolly. "I lend my weapons to no man."

Over the table Watson told us the swamp lasted for only a few more miles, and then the road would lead through the forest.

Inside my shirt I could feel the oil-skin packet and my curiosity was a burning thing. Yet I must be alone when the packet was opened. The other papers had dried by the heat of my body, and they, too, might be revealing.

Jambe-de-Bois came to sit beside me at the table. "It

would be a good thing," he suggested, "if we travelled together."

"Yes?"

"It would be safer, I think."

"For you or for me?"

"For both. I do not like the look of some of these," his gesture took in the others in the room, and he kept his voice low, "and I'm guessing you agree."

Why would he think me suspicious? Had he been awake during the night? Or was he, himself, the one who loomed over me and then vanished so swiftly? With that wooden leg it seemed unlikely, however.

"If you are going my way," I said, "why not?"

Not until the others had gone did we gather our possessions to leave. When my pack was firmly settled and I had taken up my tools and rifle, I turned to Watson.

"Back up the trail four or five miles there is a dead man. He was a British officer, and someone will be looking for him.

"Take this," I handed him a coin from the dead man's small store, "and see the body is properly buried on dry land. His name was Captain Robert Foulsham, and it was yesterday he died . . . put his name and the date of death upon the marker."

Bett was staring at me, her eyes level and hard. Watson took the coin, then said, "How did he die?"

"He was murdered," I replied, "stabbed and he either fell or was thrown into the swamp. He lived long enough to tell me these things."

"Murdered? But who—?"

"I think one of those who slept the night, that was

why I said nothing. Had I told you before there might well have been another killing."

"His possessions?"

"He had little. I shall write to his family and his superiors, and they will come to be sure he is buried well." I paused. "So please see to it."

We stepped off at a good pace for I no longer worried about the peg-legged man keeping up. During my talk with Watson, he had said nothing.

Alone upon the trail he said, "You take risks, my friend. There are some things better left alone."

"Perhaps, but I am not one to let things lie. I shall inform those who should be informed, and then go about my business."

"It may not be so easy. Once a thing like this begins, who knows when it will end? Or where?"

We walked under the perpetual gloom of interlaced boughs that shut out all but scattered bits of daylight. The earth beneath was black, a mass of rotted and rotting vegetation. Leaves lay upon stagnant pools, fallen logs thrust up ugly heads tangled with a weaving of twisted roots around which the black water gathered.

It was a mixture of oak, beech, walnut and basswood, great old trees, shadowed and still. Back into the forest all was dark and a gloom impenetrable. The trail was barely passable. This far along the corduroy logs had not been replaced, and every step was a risk of life and limb. At last we reached firm ground, higher ground. The cold wind started up again, rustling the leaves and chilling us as it blew down the long dark aisle.

Several times I saw blazed trees, evidently to indicate where lay the road when all was covered with snow. The swamp was skimmed with ice. Once we passed the ruin of a cabin, a worn fence close by, the bark falling from the poles, rank grass growing up to cover all that lay upon the ground, and to make the cabin seem even more lost and lonely.

We walked, and as we walked, we talked of many things, of ships and men and storms at sea, of wrecks and ship's timbers, and the building of strong craft and the feel of a well-made ship in a heavy sea. I had been out upon the Gulf many a time, and had once sailed to Newfoundland, Nova Scotia and Labrador. When no more than ten I had sailed alone to Bonaventure Island which lay within sight of my home. But these were things many a lad from Gaspe had done. Although I was no seafaring man, I knew how to build a ship and what it took to make one seaworthy.

Jambe-de-Bois was more. He was a deep water sailorman, and had sailed as bos'n, sail-maker and as a ship's carpenter. He spoke of Marseilles, La Rochelle and Dieppe, of St. Malo, Bristol and Genoa. He knew the Malabar Coast, the Irrawaddy and Taku Bar. Much of what he talked about I had heard of in my childhood, for many a Talon had returned from the sea, or worked, as I had, in the trades of ships and shipping.

Suddenly, I stopped. We had rounded a turn in what passed for a road and there a few hundred yards away were Macklem and his companions.

Jambe-de-Bois swore under his breath, but it was too late, for he had seen us and stopped to wait.

"Be careful, lad!" Jambe-de-Bois said, "yon's an evil

man, and one without moral or mercy. Give him the slightest chance and he'll have your heart out."

"You know him then?"

He was silent, as if he had said too much, and then he replied, bitterly. "Aye, know him I do . . . or of him, and an ugly thing it was when first he passed my bows.

"Watch yourself, and trust him not for one minute. For some reason you've attracted his interest, and those who interest him die. I've seen it happen."

Colonel Rodney Macklem waited for us on the trail, a bold and handsome man.

CHAPTER III

"QUICKLY, LAD, BEFORE we come up to him, and speak low for sound carries . . . where are you bound?"

Hesitate I did. Who was he to ask me this? Could I trust him more than Macklem, who seemed the most complete gentleman? Well, I had to trust someone. Though no doubt a formidable opponent in the right sort of fight, I had a hard time imagining Jambe so easily besting a man like Captain Foulsham or having the dexterity of the man who tried to rob me the night before.

"We've more in common than you think, much more. He wants you dead, lad, and me also. Together we're no match for him, but we might last longer. What say you?"

"I am going to Pittsburgh."

He scowled. "Pittsburgh? Where is that?"

We slowed our walk and spoke softly, "It's a new town in the west. There was a fort there once, Fort Pitt. It is a place where rivers meet and where they build boats for use on the western waters."

"Western waters? The Pacific?"

"No . . . the rivers. There are great rivers there, rivers that go every which way. Do you know the Mississippi?"

"Aye, I've shipped into New Orleans a time or two."

"Well, there's a longer river, far longer, a river that flows into the Mississippi. It's called the Missouri. It stretches far to the westward, and begins in the Rockies. They'll be building boats in Pittsburgh to use on the western waters and, in good time, I'd like to build my own."

"If it's water you want, why not go to sea? There's places out there, islands and harbors and such that no man has seen, and many worth seeing again. Why sail a river."

"Ah, but Jambe! This is a different river! The waters flow down from the high peaks, down through roaring canyons, it's a river that is nearly three thousand miles long, and who knows what may lie at its head or along its banks? I shall build a steamboat, Jambe, a steamboat that will climb to its farthest reaches. If you wish to come with me, I can use a partner, but I want no fair-weather friend. If you sign on with me it's for the voyage, or be damned."

Jambe-de-Bois was silent, finally he swore, irritably. "Oh, why not? I'll come along, John Daniel . . . if that is what you call yourself . . . for I've a thought we'll be safer together."

We came up to Macklem then, standing in the road with three others of the past night, the snake-eyed man among them.

"Come along," he said cheerfully, "there's safety in numbers and I hear the Indians can still be dangerous at times, to say nothing of thieving white men."

So we went along together, Macklem and myself in the lead, and Jambe-de-Bois falling back to bring up the rear, but in such a position that if any attempt was made upon me he would be first to see a false move and not only warn but aid me. Yet there was a rankling doubt in me, for what did I know of him?

I was among those who seemed to be enemies, yet there was a youthful foolishness and confidence in me that made me believe I could win out even if it came to blows with the lot of them. I was stronger than they likely realized, and a better shot . . . yet there was enough good sense in me despite my vanity to realize I might get no chance to shoot, nor even to use my strength.

Gradually the trees thinned out, farms appeared, and toward evening boys or girls driving cattle home from the pasture. People stopped to watch us go by, some answered our friendly hails, and some did not, yet all stared, strangers were an uncommon sight.

THE INN, when we came to it, was not like the hovel in which we had stopped before. It was a spacious place with two floors, several glass windows, and a common room where drinks and food were served.

The proprietor here was a man of dignity, who spoke of politics in a manner that sounded as if he knew of what he spoke, but I was not sure. Perhaps he was no more than a fat wind-bag. There were a-plenty of them about in that year of 1821. Yet the linens were fresh, the floors swept, the food excellently prepared.

Alone in my room, with the doors locked and hot water in the tub that had been brought for me, I bathed . . . the first time since leaving Quebec and only the second since leaving my home in the Gaspe. There are no bathing facilities in swamps and forests, nor in the piercing cold weather that had accompanied us most of the distance.

The papers I had taken from the pocket of Captain Foulsham were almost illegible. One was a letter, apparently from a brother. I could make out but little of it as water had blurred the ink and made it run. The brother lived in London, and was urging Captain Foulsham to return.

Seated at a small table, the windows still rimmed with steam from the tub, I wrote to the address of his brother in England. Carefully, I stated just what I had found, and how I had come upon the body of Captain Foulsham. I also related how I had gone through the pockets and retrieved what was there, and that the money would be forwarded to him.

Moreover, I informed him I was quite sure the murderer was either one of the party that had come along from that time to this, or that the murderer was known to one or more of them. Each I described with care, adding such fragments as might be useful, then I took it upon myself to open the oil-skin packet.

In the packet was an order for the arrest of one Baron Richard Torville, a deserter from the British army, a traitor. There was also information to the effect that Torville had been an agent for certain forces in France against Bonaparte, but that he had committed a murder and absconded with money that did not belong to him.

It was a long bill, listing a half-dozen crimes. The picture that emerged was of a shrewd man, unprincipled and dangerous, but one with powerful connections. The title by which he was known was itself borrowed without right . . . there was even doubt about his name. The past of the man was shrouded in mystery.

However, there was no physical description.

Foulsham, as an agent of His Majesty's government, had somehow tracked down and located the man, and had been murdered. And now I found myself in possession of information that could lead to my own death.

Putting all the papers in a packet I returned them to my shirt and went down to the common room.

It was empty.

In a small study opening off the common room I found Simon Tate, the proprietor.

"Sir," I closed the door. "I have a matter of urgency and secrecy."

He picked up his glasses and stared at me, putting down his pen. That he was doubtful was obvious, but taking from my pocket the small stack of gold coins, I placed them on the table.

"I would like a draft for those, and a receipt."

He eyed the money and then me. Briefly, giving only the barest details, I told him of the body, that Captain Robert Foulsham was a man of importance, and that the money was to be returned to his family and the papers likewise.

That Tate was a man of affairs was obvious. His questions were few and to the point, and in a matter of minutes I was leaving the room with a receipt tucked away in my wallet.

At the door Tate stopped me. Wind-bag he might seem when talking at large in the common room, but he was serious now. "This man of whom you speak," he said quietly, "is a dangerous man. Once a man engages in political intrigue it can become a way of life. You must ask yourself as I now am, why is he *here*? Such a man does not only think of escape . . . you can be sure he has other ideas." He paused, "Mr. Talon, I must speak of this to a friend of mine."

This I did not like, yet I hesitated. "What sort of friend?"

"You might say that he has the ear of those who matter. He is a man who seems of no importance, yet when he speaks, those in power listen."

"Very well then."

"A moment, Mr. Talon. You have chosen to confide in me, and you have acted . . . you have acted correctly, I believe, so let us talk, just for a minute.

"I know too little of affairs in your country, but I would assume they are similar to ours. Let us simply say that here the people rule . . . but to rule is not enough. The people must also be watchful, they must care for their country and its future.

"There are many self-seekers amongst us, yet even many of those are sincere patriots. Our country is growing, and there are many forces, some abroad, some within, that are dangerous to us. You know of the purchase of the Louisiana Territory?"

"I have heard of it."

"Its borders are ill-defined. We have Spain for a neighbor on the west and we have Great Britain on the north and west. I know that some of the British and most of the Canadians are our friends . . . but some are not.

"What we have most to fear, I believe, are those within our own borders who think less of country than of themselves, who are ambitious for money, for power, for land. Some of these men would subvert anything . . . anything at all, my dear sir, for their own profit. They would even twist the laws of their own country in their desire to acquire wealth and power. Such men are always prepared to listen to a smooth talking man with a proposal.

"Are you going to stay among us, Mr. Talon?"

"I do not know," I said frankly. "I have come to this country because there seemed to be opportunity. Like us all I am looking for . . . success, I suspect. Money, perhaps. I have heard they are building boats at Pittsburgh. I am a builder."

He nodded. "Good! Very good! We need builders, sir. We need them very much, but we need builders who build not only for themselves and for profit . . . and I certainly believe in profit . . . but for the future. Are you that kind of a builder, Mr. Talon?"

To tell the truth, I had not thought of it. Yet I suspected I was . . . or hoped I was. Politics had never entered my life or my thinking, nor had it seemed that the government of a people was any part of my consideration. Suddenly, uneasily, I began to realize that it might be . . . that it was.

"I hope so, Mr. Tate."

"Exactly. You must remember, my friend, that if we leave the governing to others, then others will govern, and possibly not as we would like it. In a country such as this none of us is free of responsibility."

"Yes, sir."

"What I am getting at, Mr. Talon, is that you have inadvertently come upon something that may be of great importance, and in which you are already involved. It might be very helpful if you would keep an eye on the situation . . . tactfully, of course."

"I don't see how I could do that. My only concern is

to go west and find a job building boats for the western waters. I have no interest in politics or intrigue."

He studied me for a moment, then shrugged. "So be it. However, young man, you find yourself involved. If what you have told me is true, the murderer of the young officer may have been someone very close to you. He may suspect you have or had these papers. And he may attempt murder to recover them.

"It has been said that the guilty flee when none pursueth, Mr. Talon, but the guilty often suspect others of knowing more than they do. Your own life may be in jeopardy."

"I shall have to risk that. I have little choice in the matter."

"And remember, sir, that although you are not at present a citizen here that you cannot achieve success if there is turmoil or revolution or war. Good government is everybody's business."

I shrugged. "I know nothing of that. I am simply a builder."

He got to his feet. "I hope you continue to be so, Mr. Talon. Good luck to you."

When I closed the door behind me I stood for a minute, I felt that somehow I had come off as less than I wished. Yet what business was it of mine?

That question did not give me any sense of relief. There was much to what Tate had said, that good government was the responsibility of us all. Even to me, an alien and a stranger.

Jambe-de-Bois was waiting outside the door, soaking up the morning sunlight. He squinted up at me, one lid half-lowered. "They left. Rode off down the road. Macklem . . . he asked about you."

Macklem was gone, that was good, yet how far had he gone? And it was not he so much as the snake-eyed man of whom I thought. Were they together? Or had they, like Jambe-de-Bois and myself, simply fallen in together because they travelled in a similar direction?

My thoughts returned to my tools. I should get a horse or a mule . . . or a horse and a mule.The tools had grown very heavy, and the distance was far. Yet, if I could reach a river, I could put together my own boat and simply float down to Pittsburgh or its vicinity, for I had only the vaguest idea of where Pittsburgh was.

Mentally, I reviewed my finances and decided to walk.

And then I saw the girl.

CHAPTER IV

SHE WAS YOUNG, she was lovely, and she was riding a spirited chestnut gelding which she handled with superlative ease. Beside her rode two men.

One was middle-aged and stalwart of build, a man with sandy hair now going gray. He had a broad face, a hard jaw, and the look about him of a Scotsman. The second man was younger, slightly built and good-looking, though somewhat overdressed for a ride in the woods. Both men were armed, both rode good horses.

They came right up to the inn door and the girl looked at me, "Young man, may I speak to the host?"

Something in her supercilious manner irritated me. "You may if you like," I said quietly. "He's right inside."

Her face flushed ever so lightly, and I was not sure whether it was embarrassment or anger.

"Would you call him for me, please?"

"Of course." Put that way, how could I refuse.

Stepping inside, I called out, "Mr. Tate? A lady to see you."

He came to the door, and his broad face immediately broke into a smile. "Miss Majoribanks! A pleasure, would you step down, please? We'll have a bit of something put on for you."

He held up a hand for her and she stepped down,

lightly, gracefully, gathering her skirt as she moved to the door.

"Have you heard from your brother, Miss Majoribanks?"

She stopped. "No, Mr. Tate, I have not. That is why I am here."

She passed inside, and he followed. Her two companions dismounted, the older one throwing me a quick glance that seemed to measure me and take me in completely, and then same for Jambe. On him his eyes lingered a bit.

The younger man got down also. "If you ask me," he said to the older man, "this is a fool's errand. If Charles were alive he would have returned, and if he is not alive, what good can we do?"

"He is her brother," the older man replied stiffly. "She will do what she can, as her father would have done."

"I still say it is foolish."

"Perhaps, but she will do as she pleases, you know that. And if I were you, I'd not attempt to dissuade her."

He shrugged. "I tried, for all the good it did me. She will not listen."

They tied their horses and hers to the hitching rail and went inside. For a moment I sat still, their words meant nothing to me for l knew none of them nor their problems but I had never seen a girl who made me want to look again as this one had. Amused, yet unable to deny myself, I went inside and sat at a table near the window. Tate glanced at me, a little surprised, I thought. I ordered a glass of cider merely to look at the girl again.

Obviously, she lived not too far away, for she was

known to Simon Tate, and I suspected that she stopped here often.

"Mr. Tate," she was saying, "the last we heard from Charles was from St. Louis. He was planning to go up the Missouri . . . that's a river out there . . . with a group of government men, scientists and surveyors. That was months ago."

"You must understand," Tate suggested, "that mails are slow, and the expedition may have not yet returned."

"I do understand. The letter was received by me three months ago, but it had been written some time before that." She looked directly at him. "Mr. Tate, I believe that letter was purposely delayed."

"Purposely?" He was obviously puzzled. "But why? Who would have reason to delay a letter from a young man to his sister?"

"Because that young man had suddenly come upon some information someone did not wish him to have, and having it, they did not wish anyone informed.

"I know my brother's seal. His ring is new. This seal had been broken and re-sealed. In other words, the letter had been read by someone else, and forwarded to me only when they decided the contents were innocent enough."

"Please, Miss Majoribanks, aren't you imagining this? I mean, your brother is an ambitious student. He is a naturalist of particular skill . . . but he has a way of becoming deeply involved in his work, of losing himself in it. I believe you should have patience."

"I spoke of information, Mr. Tate. My brother is in serious trouble, and may have been murdered or held prisoner. I mean to go west and find out for myself."

"Please, please!" Tate protested. "This is all romance. You have no knowledge—"

"But I do! Mr. Tate, when my brother and I were very young we used to play all sorts of games, war games, capture games, games of plots against the Republic . . . you know how children are. Most of them were wildly imaginative, and we invented a country, 'our' country, we called it. We called it, and I don't know where he got the name or how he invented it, we called it 'Iggisfeld.' "

"I understand, but—"

"You do *not* understand. Please listen. There was a girl next door whom we both detested, and somehow she learned of our game, eavesdropping, I suspect, and teased us about it. Her name was Pucinara . . . I mean, it really was. So, Pucinara became a name, our name, for the enemy.

"Mr. Tate . . . please, read this." She handed him a sheet of paper.

Simon Tate took the paper, and fortunately for me, he read aloud.

After some brief account of his health, travels and general condition, Charles Majoribanks listed a dozen or so of plants by their common or botanical names, and followed with several butterflies and spiders observed. Then he added, "*You will be interested to know that I have come upon a particularly dangerous infection, a form of the Pucinara, which if left unchecked will be a grave danger to Iggisfeld. I must follow this up and, if not prevented, will forward my conclusions to you for you will know those scholars best able to deal with this material.*"

Simon Tate paused when he had finished reading, then re-read the message again to himself.

"So, I have come to you, Mr. Tate," she said. "You are also a man with wide knowledge of affairs, and know what should be done about this."

Tate looked at the message again, then he looked at her. "What do you believe it means?"

"Mr. Tate, the plants and other wild life listed were all known to my brother before he left home. There would be no purpose in sending me such a list except to lend obscurity to what follows, which is the real message.

"My brother has come upon some plot, some action or people whom he believes are dangerous to the country. This is his way of communicating the information to us. Obviously, he suspected his letter would be opened and read, and he wished it to sound harmless while yet telling us what he wished us to know."

Tate stared thoughtfully at the letter, then he said, "Miss Majoribanks, you have yourself said this letter is some months old . . . and perhaps was delayed and so may be even older. Yet nothing has happened. Nor do I see any possibility of danger arising in such a remote area. It seems to me—"

"Mr. Tate, the Louisiana Territory once belonged to France. It also belonged to Spain. There are those in both countries who might regret that it has fallen into our hands.

"There is rebellion in Mexico and I know enough of what is happening in New Orleans to know that every loose-footed adventurer in that part of the world is gathering there or in St. Louis or Pittsburgh or Lexington . . . expecting something to happen."

"You seem well-informed."

She was intelligent, and she was assured. I was surprised to see how assured, yet when she continued to talk, I could see why she had reason to be.

"Mr. Tate, you knew my father?"

"Of course. I respected him very much, a very astute businessman and trader. He made few mistakes."

"He made no mistakes. That was because he had information, and he took care to see that his news was not only the latest but the best."

"How do you mean?"

"Mr. Tate, did you ever hear of the Fuggers?"

"Yes . . . I believe so. Weren't they merchants of some sort?"

"They were. Merchants, money-lenders, men who financed trade and even financed Charles V, an emperor, and one of the most powerful men of his time.

"The Fuggers began as simple weavers, Mr. Tate. They were peasants, weaving in their cottages, and then in the 14th century, one of them decided to become a merchant. Within a few years they achieved great wealth, partly because one of them created fustian, a weaving of cotton and linen, but mostly because they gathered information.

"They were a large family, and soon scattered over Europe, but, they exchanged information, their agents sent them information, and their ship captains did likewise. The major reason for their wealth and power was because they always knew a good deal more than those with whom they dealt.

"If there was a crop failure in Russia, they knew it. If a ship with a valuable cargo sank off the coast of Greece, they were the first to hear of it. They knew what was to be in surplus and what was likely to be scarce, and they bought or sold accordingly."

"But what has this to do with us?"

"Simply, that my father took a leaf from their book. He financed traders among the Indians, had friends among the soldiers, among the flat-boat men, among the itinerant preachers. He received letters from all over the country, letters that told him who was going where and what was happening.

"There was nothing mysterious about it. He wrote letters and he requested answers, he even paid for information, but most of it was just an exchange of ideas. At the time of my father's death he had over one hundred correspondents in this country and in Europe."

"I see."

"You *begin* to see, Mr. Tate. This correspondence grew too large for my father to handle, so my brother and I helped. We opened the letters, read them, listed the information in ledgers and passed the most important letters on to my father.

"Since my father's death I have continued this correspondence. Despite the fact that we no longer live in New York or Boston, the letters have come, and I have maintained contact with all these sources and have helped to operate my father's business."

"I was not aware of that."

"We have excellent managers. They never knew the source of my father's information, nor have I told anyone but you. I have continued to advise them as to buying and selling, and we have continued to profit."

"And you have information that something is wrong out west?"

"Let us say I had grounds for suspicion, and then this letter from my brother. When I received it, I got out the ledgers and read all the information we had on the Louisiana Territory, read the reports of Lewis and Clark, and letters from James Mackay. My father had an agent in Santa Fe for more than thirty years, Mr. Tate, I read his reports.

"Then I read letters from New Orleans, from Madrid, from Paris and La Rochelle. What my brother has discovered is a plot to seize the Louisiana Territory and to make an independent kingdom of it."

"That's nonsense."

She shrugged. "Exactly the reaction from our senator, Mr. Tate. I approached him on the matter. He either does not believe anything I say or has reasons for not wishing to believe."

"Miss Majoribanks, you must remember, you are a very *young* lady. You are in fact—?"

"Nineteen, Mr. Tate, and for all those years I sat at my father's knee. For most of that time I have had access to his office. I learned how to read from those letters of his. It was not only crop failures or successes that interested my father. A knowledge of political change is very essential to the conduct of international business . . . or any business, for that matter."

"That may be, but—"

"I know you have connections of your own. I know some of your political affiliations. I have told you all this not only to give you my reasons for going west but because I hoped you will see the necessity for prompt action.

"Mr. Tate, the man who is to direct the movements in

the Louisiana Territory may already be en route. I know much of the man, and he will stop at nothing."

Tate smiled, shrugging. "Your worry about our country does you credit, but that is a vast and empty land out yonder. It is highly likely any such move could be made. They would need an army, supplies, arms."

"They will have them."

"Miss Majoribanks, if half of what you suggest be true, it would be utter folly for you to go west. Your brother is a man of judgment. He will handle his own situation, and you can do nothing but make it more difficult for him. Also, despite your information I think you have exaggerated fears. No man would have the audacity or the skill to attempt such a thing."

"Baron Torville would."

CHAPTER V

"TORVILLE!" I almost dropped my glass, and I am a man not easily startled.

She turned to look at me, seeming to be aware of my presence for the first time. "You have been eavesdropping on a conversation that is no concern of yours!" she said sharply.

"I beg your pardon," I replied, "I am drinking my cider. It was impossible not to overhear your conversation."

Simon Tate glanced at me, started to speak, then let the moment slide. Both the men who accompanied her looked over at me, the younger with obvious disapproval, the older with a careful, measuring look.

The conversation continued, but in lower tones and I heard nothing more that made sense, yet I needed little more. Haughty the young lady might be, but she was obviously well-informed, and I had great respect for her sources of information. My family knew all about the Fuggers . . . my ancestor had dealings with them, and may even have written some of those letters of which she spoke. In fact, he had himself used somewhat the same methods to keep abreast of changing situations in India, China, and the Malay Archipelago.

If the young lady's information was correct, Torville was the leader or one of the leaders of some sort of a plot to seize the Louisiana Territory and set up an independent kingdom. It seemed a wild scheme, yet there were many reasons why it might be successful. Not until 1818 had a firm boundary been established between the United States and Canada along the 49th parallel from the Rainy Lake to the Rockies. Earlier in the year a treaty had been signed with Spain ceding Florida to the United States and defining the western border of the Louisiana Purchase at the 42nd parallel and the United States had renounced claims to Texas.

All that would seem to have clarified matters somewhat but actually many Americans believed reports from various officers of the Army that the great plains were a vast wasteland, the so-called Great American Desert, and so totally unfit for cultivation or settlement. The result was that few Americans believed the area worth fighting for . . . yet others saw those empty lands as the very definition of opportunity.

In Mexico there had been an ongoing struggle for independence from Spain and the prospects of fighting had lured adventurers and soldiers-of-fortune from all over the world. Many had gathered in New Orleans to await the turn of events that might offer them opportunity for sudden wealth, looting, or whatever chance might offer. Rumors of gold in the western lands, mostly coming from Santa Fe and from Mexico itself, had lured others.

Moreover, the changing status of the slave trade had caused a number of slavers to abandon the sea. In 1808 a law had been passed forbidding the importation of slaves into the United States, and even now a bill was before Congress that would make foreign slave trade an act of piracy punishable by death. With the influence of slave holders within the British empire having been greatly diminished by the American revolution, the English abolitionists seemed ready to lead the fight on the high seas. Although the smuggling of slaves might continue, many of those traders who wished to take no chances were looking for a fresh area to make their fortunes. Much of this I knew from shore-side gossip in the Gaspe where the sailors arriving from Charleston, Boston, Jamaica and Antigua were constantly arguing such questions in the grog shops along the waterfront. Jambe-de-Bois had, during our long walk down through Maine, also talked of this.

The captains and owners of former slave ships, while looking for a new use of their talents and equipment, were apt to be too cautious to become embroiled in any such schemes as that of Torville's, yet that was not true of their crews, a rough, lawless and cut-throat lot.

Finishing my cider, I got up, paid what I owed and went out. The older man with Miss Majoribanks followed me.

"Mister? M' name is Macaire. I do be wantin' a word wi' you."

I liked him. There seemed a broad and straightforward honesty to the man.

"Mine is John Daniel," I said, carrying on with the name I'd given before.

"Y' spoke of Torville. Or y' seemed to ken the name."

So, I explained, as briefly as possible, the finding of the body and the papers.

"Y' said nothing of the murder at the inn?"

"I did not . . . not until the others had gone. There were some there I did not like the look of."

He kicked at the post of the hitching rail, as he considered what I'd said. "They be some're around here then?" he muttered.

"The men who were at the inn with me went south. There's a snake-eyed one . . . I'd not trust him. But I know none of them."

"Aye, I will speak to the Miss of it."

"Don't tell her it comes from me . . ." I said, "I have an idea she took offense."

He chuckled. "Likely! She's a proud one! But a fine, fine lass!" He looked at me. "You'll not be stayin' on here?"

"It's no place for a shipwright," I said. "I shall go where the building is."

"Aye," he agreed, "it is a fine thing, to work with wood, an' there's a deal of it here. The finest maple, oak or beech. To build . . . aye, I like that . . . it is good to build."

He held out his hand. "Well, lad, here's luck to you. May the road lie easy wherever you walk."

"And the same to you," I said.

Jambe-de-Bois had come up, and said, "There's no horse to be had here, but perhaps in the village yonder."

"We'll walk that way," I said.

Simon Tate came to the door as we started to move off. "You will go now?"

"Aye."

He walked over to me. His face was serious. "I will not be sending your papers. I will take them on myself. There is a smell to this I do not like."

"Be careful, then."

We parted, and with Jambe-de-Bois I walked toward

the village. Walking opens the mind to thought, and when serious problems beset me, I walk and let my mind ramble, exploring the problem at hand.

Torville was not far from my thoughts, although I intended to get about my business. There were officials and all manner of men whose business it was to see to such criminals and revolutionaries. The man was probably over-rated in his villainy and, regardless, was certainly nothing for the likes of me to be worrying about.

But my thoughts swung away from the current in which I wished them to go to muse about that girl, Miss Majoribanks. Much as she did not care for me, I found myself admiring her direct, head-on approach to things, although I thought her foolish to go into the west looking for a brother who might well be in no trouble at all. Mails were an uncertain thing, and many of those to whom letters were trusted were themselves careless about delivery, and apt to stop for a drink or two . . . or three or four.

The village was a neat cluster of buildings, a store, a blacksmith shop, a small tavern and a horse-barn.

"We'll say nothing about wanting a horse or mule," I said, "we'll stop for a drink, and talk of the way ahead."

A half-dozen men loitered outside the inn. One was a large-bellied man with a somewhat soiled shirt. He had a keen blue eye that took me in, along with my load of tools, my pack, and the wooden leg of Jambe-de-Bois.

The man looked and smelled of horses, so I walked past him to the inn, then stopped and walked back. "Is it a place for a working-man?" I asked him. "Are the prices not too strong?"

"Reasonable," he commented, "reasonable." He glanced

at my load. "It takes a man of muscle to carry the load," he said.

"Aye," I agreed. "I bargained for a mule, but the cost was dear, and cheaper it be to carry the load m'self."

"It's a way of thinkin'," he agreed. I could see that he was of no mind to carry any such loads, and thought me a fool for so doing.

We entered the inn and seated ourselves near the window. Jambe went to the window that opened into the kitchen asking for ale.

The proprietor brought it and I paid him at once. He glanced at the coins in my hand. He nodded toward the road. "'Tis a rough road for shank's mare," he said. "You should have a horse or two."

"Dear," I shook my head, "a horse is too dear."

"You could sell it when we get where we're going," Jambe suggested.

"Yes, I could that, but I have no horse and I doubt much if this village has a horse for sale, or a mule."

The large-bellied man came in and glanced our way. He collected a mug of cider and sat down, straddling a chair so he could lean on the back. "Mind if I join you?" he asked.

I grinned at him. "You already have, but seeing you brought your own drink, you're welcome."

The dealer chuckled. "You'd not buy me a drink, then?"

"When a man comes to sell me a horse, I think he should buy the drinks."

The dealer chuckled again. "Wise, ain't you? Well, young feller, I'm not saying I'd refuse a deal. And a fine, prosperous lad like yourself . . . well, it's a bit rough for you to walk the country carrying such a load of tools."

"I'm strong."

"Aye," the dealer admitted, "I can see that. We've a couple of powerful lads about here. Too bad you're passin' . . . we might arrange us a bout of wrestling." The dealer looked at me with narrowed eyes, "You do wrestle?"

"Well—" I hesitated, long enough to seem doubtful, "I suppose I could." No reason to let him know I'd thrown dozens of young men in Quebec and Nova Scotia and a few in Newfoundland. There's a good bit of friendly grappling done in the seaport towns, and in going from one to the other there'd been fairs and such.

Of course, I'd had good training. The best in fact, for it was a tradition in our family since the first Talon, who had learned to grapple and roll in India, China and Japan. He had trained his sons well, and father and son since, we had all learned Eastern and Cornish styles as well as something of the boxing such as they do in Britain. But there was no need to say aught of that.

"There's those about always ready for a bit of sport," the dealer commented. "There's a local man . . . Neely Hall. He wins most of the time. He's beaten everybody about here but Sam Purdy . . . and of course, nobody wrestles Purdy."

"This Purdy, is he so good then?" Jambe-de-Bois asked.

"*Good?* He'd make two of the lad here, and he's got the power to match his size. There was a wrestler came through here two months ago. He'd defeated everybody, and Purdy tossed him in a moment. He's a giant, Purdy is, doesn't know his own strength."

Now such talk nettled me a little. I shifted uneasily in my seat. There was no man invincible, not even me, and big men always got under my skin a little. That is, if they were the aggressive, bullying type. I had no idea that Purdy was, but such talk of invincibility stirred something in me. We also needed horses and this might be a way to afford more than we could otherwise pay for.

"What if I wrestled him," I said mildly, "just for fun, you know."

The horse-dealer laughed. "Fun? With Purdy? It would be no fun, lad. He's rough. When you wrestle with Purdy it's anything-goes . . . you can gouge or bite if you're of a mind to, although the last man to try biting Purdy left here with no teeth in the front of his face.

"No, no. I wasn't thinking of Purdy. It was Neely Hall. I don't think you're up to him, but it might be a match. The boys would come out to see it, and there'd be some betting done."

He looked at me. "Do y' bet, lad? Or have y' scruples again it?"

"Well . . . if it isn't for too much. After all, I don't know this man Hall, and I'm a stranger. There mightn't be fair-play."

"Oh, there'll be fair-play!" the dealer said. "They are honest boys about here. There's sporting blood, but it's honest sporting blood."

Jambe-de-Bois looked at the dealer, a baleful gleam in his eyes.

"They'd be honest," he said coolly, "I'd be sure of that."

The dealer looked at Jambe uneasily. It was a quiet comment, but there was an under-current of iron in it, and looking at the one-legged man the dealer felt a momentary icy shiver as if somebody had stepped on his grave.

"Would you be for it?" the dealer turned to me. "There's been nothing doing about here for weeks, now."

"Well . . . I'm just passing through," I said. "I had not thought of it, nor stopping. It is a far way I have to go."

"Stay. Neely is about, and it could be done for tomorrow. If you've a little money for betting—"

"Well. You were talking of a horse. I had not thought of one but maybe . . . well, maybe I should use the money and a bit more I have to buy a horse or two. We've far to go."

It was Purdy I wanted, but it was plain to see I'd have to go through this Neely Hall to get to him. And I might just get a horse in the process.

"We'd best go," I said to Jambe-de-Bois. "I make no boast of being one to wrestle in a match. I've only have tussled with boys . . . I don't think so."

"Come, now!" The dealer wanted his bit of sport, after all, what was there to do in a settlement of forty people with maybe fifty others within an hour's ride? "Nobody will get hurt. It is just a friendly match."

He got up quickly. "Enjoy your drinks, lads, and be havin' another on me. I'll talk to the boys."

When he was gone, Jambe-de-Bois studied me with some care. "You're surely knowin' some of these country lads are strong? They wrestle a bit of an evenin' and about the fairs. It'll be no easy thing to do . . . if you do. Have you wrestled at all?"

"Here and there. When I was a boy in school—"

"A boy in school," Jambe-de-Bois was contemptuous. "This will not be like that, and you'll be getting yourself hurt for no reason."

"I want a horse," I said quietly. "In fact, I want three of them . . . or mules. I want one for me, one for you, and another for the packs. So, finish your drink, and we'll be over the way to look at the horses."

"You're going to bet?"

"Aye. I'll bet."

He was silent, and as for myself, I was remembering that the breadth of my shoulders could cause me to look shorter than I am, and the fact that every bit of me was solidly packed muscle over bone made me look fifteen pounds lighter than I actually was. This was in my favor, that and the fact that they knew nothing of me.

But it was Sam Purdy I wanted; that was where we would make our money.

CHAPTER VI

FINE HORSES THERE were in the lot, a couple of handsome geldings and a likely-looking mare, but it was not these of which I was thinking. There was a stallion, too, but a stallion along the country lanes and in the villages can cause a man a deal of trouble.

What took my eye was a couple of sturdy, hair-legged geldings rough with their winter coats. Neither was over thirteen hands but they had strong, well-muscled shoulders and power in their haunches. And there was a sad-eyed, wise-looking mule. A black mule with whitish rings around his eyes, and when he saw me studying him he tossed his head and yawned.

Jambe-de-Bois studied them with an unfriendly eye. "I'll have you know I'm no good a-settin' the dec o' one o' them," he said grimly. "I'd rather walk."

"It is not so bad, and the mule yonder could carry our packs and the tools."

"I'll abide that. It's settin' one o' them takes me down."

We walked back to the inn and resumed our former table. The host came over to us. He looked at me, measuring my shoulders with a careful eye. "You're taking on a bit," he commented, "Neely is a likely lad, strong and a good wrestler."

"He's big, is he?"

"Bigger than you by thirty pound. He's beaten them all but Purdy. Nobody can beat Purdy," the inn-keeper was quite serious. "He's cruel, a cruel, bitter man who fights to wound or injure. There's those about who'd give a lot to see him whipped."

"It will come. If I beat Neely, I shall try him."

"You?" The inn-keeper was scornful. "He would eat you alive."

It irritated me, this talk of the invincible Purdy. But the inn-keeper crossed to the side-board and came back with a piece of iron. It was a horseshoe that had straightened. "What d' you think o' that? He did that here before us all, while we looked on, it was."

Taking it from him I looked at it, shaking my head. "You are right, of course, it took a man to bend that." Then I looked up. "The horse-dealer promised us another drink. Could we have it now?"

When he was gone, I put the straightened horseshoe down on the table and when he returned I said, "We'll eat now, for I want my food to settle before I grapple with Neely Hall."

"You will meet him, then?"

"I will."

"You'll be stayin' the night then?"

"We will, so mark us down for two good beds."

When we had eaten, we pushed back from the table, and when Jambe-de-Bois turned toward the door and nobody was looking, I took the iron horseshoe and bent it double, almost back to its former shape. Glancing at it, I applied a bit more pressure, and when the inn-keeper stopped by our table I held it down by my side. "Your food is good," I said, "the ale excellent, and between us two, I think you're a likely man. But if you are also a wise one who likes to make a bit of money on the side, you'll say nothing of this to anyone."

He looked puzzled, wondering of what I was speaking. Then I handed him his horseshoe.

He started to speak, then abruptly he closed his mouth and went to the side-board where he thrust the shoe back into a drawer and out of sight.

The horse-dealer came in. He crossed to the table and sat down. "Neely will meet you. Right here in front of the inn at sundown. Over there on the grass, yonder."

I shrugged. "I haven't said I'd meet him. What do I get out of this?"

"You can make a bet. You can make as many bets as you like, and your friend, too." He smiled, and I could see how pleased he was with the idea. "I thought you might like to bet."

"I've a little put by," I said, with a shading of reluctance. "And of course, you have your horses."

"Horses?" He was startled. "I've said nothing about horses. I thought maybe two dollars—"

I laughed at him. "You're wasting my time. I'd bet you twenty English pounds against the stocky gray with three white feet, the dun and the mule."

His face shadowed a little, his eyes became worried. "I wasn't thinkin' about no such bet. I was thinkin' . . . well, just a sportin' bet, a fun bet—"

My contempt was obvious. "Sorry. You make a sporting bet and I get my nose rubbed in the dirt, fun for you . . . but what about me? Forget it."

"You won't wrassle?"

"Why should I wrestle for your fun? Sorry, my friend."

"But I done sent for Neely! I told 'em all!"

"Your problem. My offer stands. Twenty English pounds against your three animals, take it or leave it."

He shook his head, but he sat still. Leaving him with Jambe, I got up and strolled outside. Standing under the over-hang I looked up the road. Some riders had appeared on the trail, and I watched them warily.

They came closer, and I recognized Miss Majoribanks, Macaire and Simon Tate. The young man was there, too, lingering a little bit behind.

Tate reined in when he saw me. "You still here?" he stared at me in surprise.

"Well," I said, "we got involved in something. Seems they have a wrestler here, and they're trying to talk me into a bout, but this horse-dealer—"

"You mean Kimball? What about him?"

"Seems like he's a tin-horn. He wants me to wrestle, all right, but he doesn't want to bet enough to make it worthwhile gettin' dusty."

"Are you afraid?" It was that girl. She was giving me that cool, level look she had.

I shrugged. "Could be. But seeing as I have never seen the man, I doubt if I am. The one I really want is this Purdy."

"Purdy!" Tate burst out. "You'd be wrong in the head to think of it. The last man he fought lost an eye."

"He might need a lesson," I suggested.

Miss Majoribanks glared. "Well, of all the conceited—"

"Nice of you to notice, ma'am," I replied cheerfully. "But it seems they want me to fight this here Neely Hall first."

"You wouldn't have a chance. I know Neely Hall. He's very strong."

"Yes, ma'am, but when I offered to bet this Kimball twenty pounds against two horses and a mule, he backed down. I guess he doesn't think Neely's that strong anymore."

Kimball had come out of the stable. "That's not so! I'll take that bet!"

Miss Majoribanks looked down at me. "Do you have any more money?"

"I have ten pounds."

"Then I will wager with you. Fifteen pounds to your ten that Neely beats you, two falls out of three!"

"Ma'am, are you sure about that? I mean, I didn't think that—"

"You didn't think a lady would bet? Well, many have, and this one will."

"Miss?" Macaire said gently. "I wouldn't do that if I were you, you don't know this young man."

"I know him well enough to want to see Neely Hall put him in the dust!" She said abruptly, "Let's go inside."

Macaire offered her his hand and she stepped down, then went past me as if I did not exist. As she passed I caught a whiff of some faint but very pleasant perfume.

NEELY HALL CAME from his farm in a wagon. I first saw him when he stepped down in front of the inn. He was a big, hulking young man, a few years older than I and much heavier. His face had a kind of boyish softness in it which mine had lost, and he seemed a pleasant enough fellow.

He scarcely looked at me when he came in, and there were no further preliminaries. We walked out to the grass and peeled off our coats.

He moved in swiftly, then suddenly ducked and dove at my knees with the idea of up-ending me. I side-stepped quickly, pushing the side of his head as I did so, which threw him off-balance. He staggered, caught himself and came at me again.

He was quick on his feet, although his movements were clumsy and untrained, but what I wished to learn was how much he knew. Several times we grappled, and each time we broke free. The crowd had swelled to at least fifty people and Neely was performing before his friends. I began to see from his approaches that he knew the rolling hip-lock, and he also knew how to apply a head-lock or strangle-hold, for several times he seemed to be trying for these holds.

He was strong and active but I doubted if he had had twenty serious matches in his life. Moving in I reached for him but a stone rolled under my foot, and I had to shift to regain my balance. He caught me with an arm around my head and applied pressure. As he did so he tried to work his grip back so his biceps would be at my ear, his forearm across my throat.

Thrusting an arm through his spread legs I grabbed him by the buttock with one hand, dropping my left hand to his leg below the knee and bending it sharply back and clear of the ground, with a great heave I threw him over my shoulder and we both fell . . . only he lit on his head. Instantly, I spun around, dropped on him as he lay partly stunned, and pinned him to the ground.

"First fall to John Daniel!" Macaire shouted.

Holding him a moment longer to show there was no mistake, I got up.

Neely followed me, getting to his feet, staggering a little and peering at me, surprised and shaken.

Of them all I think only three knew exactly what had happened, Macaire, Simon Tate and the inn-keeper.

"I never saw that done before," Tate commented, low-voiced. "I thought he had you."

"So did he," I commented dryly.

We rested. I wiped off my face with a wet cloth, and stood waiting. Neely was across the small circle of people, getting excited advice that was undoubtedly doing more to confuse him than otherwise.

Time was called and we circled warily. He was very strong, quick, and now he was more careful. I doubt if he realized what had happened any more than the others, but he did not want it to happen again. He feinted a lunge, then lunged and caught me nappin'. He back-heeled me suddenly and I hit the ground hard on my shoulder-blade, but kicked up my feet and turned a complete somersault, coming up fast. Knowing how to fall is an art in itself, and the first training I had received as a child. How to fall, how to break one's fall, and how to rise quickly in a posture of defense.

When I'd gone down he was sure he had me and came in fast, so when I turned my somersault and came up I put my head right into a head-lock. This time I was driving hard toward him so I followed through and knocked him over backward. He took me down with him and as I broke free and started to get up he threw himself against my legs and I fell again. In an instant he was atop me. In the moment he fell upon me I had attempted to turn and he had me pinned.

"Second fall to Neely!"

I heard the shout and lay still. I had started the move that would have thrown him clear but stopped. The time was too short, but I wanted no arguments, I wanted a decisive win which could not be disputed.

We got up and I went to my side of the ring. Macaire came over to me. I was scarcely breathing hard, and simply waiting. I rinsed my mouth with water, spit it out, and mopped my face.

"You've wrestled some?" he said.

"A bit."

"Yon lad is strong, but I saw you make the move with your feet. You were going to throw up your legs and catch him under the chin with your heels and flip him off, I think."

"I was."

"Time!"

This was the decisive one, and most of my money and whether we had horses or not depended upon it. I wasted no time, wanting no accidents. I moved in quickly, then suddenly ducked and hooked an arm around his right ankle with my right arm and threw my body weight against him. He went down and I continued to roll with him, turning over atop him until I was in a perfect hold-down position with both his shoulders to the ground.

It took them a moment to realize that it was all over. The third fall had come so suddenly they were unprepared for it.

Tate came over and thrust a hand under Neely to be sure his shoulders were down, but they were. My weight was across him, and I think for the first time he realized my strength, for when he tried to move I held him still upon the ground.

"Third fall to John Daniel!"

Again I held the position until there could be no doubt, and then got up, offering a hand to Neely. He took it and got up.

"I'll buy you a cider," I said.

"Taken," he said.

We walked to the inn together, and the inn-keeper refused my money. He leaned over the bar and whispered, when Neely was turned aside, talking to a friend, "I made a bit on this, I made a good bit."

There was a light touch on my shoulder. I turned and Miss Majoribanks was there. "Your money," she said briefly. "I did not know you were a professional!"

"That I am not," I replied quietly. "I am what I seem, a man who works with wood. I wish to be no more."

"I scarcely think you need worry," she said ironically. "You have strength, enough, I suppose, but to become something needs intelligence!"

With that she turned away, her chin in the air. I was not angry, and she had a fine, proud way about her. I liked her lifted chin, and the square set of her shoulders, even the way she gathered her skirt as she turned.

"And now for Sam Purdy!" The inn-keeper said it. "But that will be a different thing, I am afraid."

"There'll be no match with Purdy," someone said, it was a new voice, and we all turned.

A man stood in the inn door, a square-set man with gaiters and a gray coat. He was an oldish man, and a gentleman by the look of him.

"No man will fight Purdy," he said.

"And why not, Reverend?" Tate asked.

"Because Sam Purdy was killed this day in Berwick, killed by the bare hands of a man to whom he spoke rudely, and then tried to thrash.

"Oh, it was a fight! For almost three minutes, it was a fight, and then the stranger killed him, dropped him with a broken neck."

"That bull neck of Sam's?" somebody said. "Oh, come now."

"He did it," the Reverend said emphatically, "did it apparently only half his mind to it. You should have seen him move! Like a cat, he was! When Sam went down he simply took out his pipe, and lighted it."

"Did this man have a name?" I asked.

"Aye," the Reverend turned to me. "He said his name was Macklem. Colonel Macklem."

CHAPTER VII

WE RODE AS a party when we left the village the next day and headed toward Berwick, a good distance down the road, if such it might be called. Miss Majoribanks and her party were in the lead, and Simon Tate rode with them. He would leave our group in Berwick and take the road down the coast to Boston town.

Jambe-de-Bois and I stayed in the rear, leaving Miss Majoribanks free of our company. She had paid off readily enough, and so had Kimball, the portly horse-dealer, although he paid off with a sour expression and bad grace.

"Lucky for you that Purdy is dead," he told me. "He would have killed you."

"He might have, but he didn't kill Macklem, did he?"

Kimball knew nothing of Macklem, but the man was much on my mind. Jambe-de-Bois had warned me of him but I had expected nothing like this. A man who could defeat, and kill, a man with a reputation like Purdy's was someone to beware of. Well, with luck, our paths had parted and we would see no more of each other. Nor had I regrets.

Tate dropped back as we neared Somersworth. "You will be going the same way as Miss Majoribanks," he suggested. "Macaire is a good man, but that other fellow . . . he doesn't measure up, although he believes he does, and she believes him."

"It is none of my affair. I shall go to Pittsburgh. What they do is their own trouble."

"But you could keep an eye on them, could you not? She's very young, John Daniel, and she is very bold and fearless . . . but she knows nothing of the world and she rides daringly into it because she has always been protected.

"If aught should happen to Macaire, I fear for her. She's like one of my own, and I have known her since childhood."

"She will have none of me. I am simply an artisan. I am not a landed man or educated—"

He glanced at me, sharply, I thought. "No? I have it on good authority that if you lived in France and had your just dues you'd be at least a Count . . . and a man of substance."

"Now who has been telling you that?" I was exasperated. "I am a simple workman. A man good with tools, and nothing more."

"Have it your own way. But you will be going at least as far as Pittsburgh. If you can help her, please do so."

"All right," I agreed.

He left us shortly after and took the coast road to Portsmouth and thence to Boston.

We, on the other hand, started south toward Haverhill, to then turn westward toward the Connecticut River. Our party was now five people. In Haverhill Miss Majoribanks expected to be joined by a companion, a lady whom she had previously known and with whom she had corresponded when she first began her plans to go west and search for her brother.

Jambe-de-Bois and I brought up the rear, riding some three horse lengths behind them, and keeping our distance.

In Berwick there was much talk of the recent fight between Sam Purdy, who had been well known in the area, and the stranger, Macklem. Too late they had considered arresting Macklem, at least for an inquiry, but he had departed the town, and nobody saw fit to pursue either him or the issue. Everyone seemed more than pleased that Purdy was out of the way with no harm done to local people.

A hostler shook his head. "Lad, I never hope to see such a thing again. I never liked Purdy. He was a rough, violent man, given to brutality, and no one was ever at ease when he was about . . . but, the way of it!

"Oh, believe me! It was the fault of Purdy! He was ugly and looking for trouble. I think he had a drink or two, and this stranger was too neat, too cool, too upstanding for his taste.

"Purdy started the trouble, but . . . well, the stranger *destroyed* him. You never saw anything like it. It was cool, deliberate, and efficient, almost without effort.

"No panting, no struggle, no cursing. He simply demolished Purdy. He must have struck him a dozen times, and a bone broken for each strike. Sometimes with fists, often with only the edge of the hand . . . but he wiped him out.

"Purdy was no coward. With a broken shoulder, the side of his face smashed in, he still tried. Then the man broke his neck. They can say what they wish . . . and most say it was an accident. I say sir, and I have seen many a fight, that Macklem knew he was going to break his neck, knew he was going to kill the man. And with not a hair mussed. He simply tucked his shirt in a bit when it was over, made some comment about self-defense, and within minutes was gone from the town."

Jambe-de-Bois listened, scowling a little. When we were away from the hostler, he said, "I told you, lad, the man is evil incarnate. We must avoid him. He will be the death of us, I tell you . . . and you, you're too confident."

I was nettled. I did not like being disposed of so lightly. At the same time, the hostler's words were shocking. It is one thing to fight, even to kill. It is another when one does it deliberately, and without hesitation or remorse.

Yet to be dismissed so lightly irritated me. I was a good fighter . . . a better fighter than the little affair with Neely Hall had showed.

When the next day came, we passed over a country which had only lately been settled although now the farm-houses were clustered more thickly together. The river ahead was crossed by a remarkable bridge of which I had heard, as had many of us who work with heavy timber. Since I had left Canada I had been expecting the crossing of it to be a highlight of my journey. Realizing we were nearly there, I took the lead and set a pace that left Jambe-de-Bois cursing both me and his mount under his breath.

The Piscataqua Bridge was a really splendid structure at least twenty-six hundred feet long, with one hundred and twenty-six piers set in the water and on the banks.

The bridge was laid out with three sections, two of them horizontal and one arched. The arch itself was said to contain seventy tons of timber. I could easily believe it, and took the time to stop, go under the bridge and examine the work. It was beautifully fitted and assembled.

We stayed the night in Exeter and not a word passed between myself and Miss Majoribanks, although Macaire was pleasant and I finally had a word or two with the younger man.

He was really quite a handsome fellow, although he had a way about him I did not trust. His name was Edwin Hale.

"I understood you were going to Boston?" he suggested.

"It was a thought we had, but I am a builder, and the western waters are the place for me."

"The western waters? Or is it Miss Majoribanks who is the attraction?"

"I have scarcely spoken to her."

He shrugged, looking at me with a sly, rather taunting smile. "You mean, she has scarcely spoken to you."

"If you prefer."

He seemed ready to provoke a quarrel so I walked away from him.

The inns we found were remarkably clean and well kept, the owners of them usually men of some importance in their communities. The food was excellent, for the most part.

At daybreak we were off and riding. As before Miss Majoribanks took off in the lead, and this time Jambe-de-Bois and I dropped even farther behind. None of the roads were good. Most were only a few years old, but were heavily rutted from rains. We kept to the grass along the shoulder and made good time. The horses I'd won in my bet with Kimball were good, stalwart animals, and at the end of the day seemed to have as much stamina as at the beginning.

We stopped to eat at high noon in the village of Kingston, eighteen miles upon our way. It was a small place of some scattered houses, a church and several stores.

Leaving Kingston, Macaire dropped back with us. We rode for several minutes and then he said suddenly, "John Daniel, are you carrying much in the way of money?"

At my obvious surprise, he said, "It is not m' business but in Kingston I come to the street afore y' an' a mon I saw. He was na one to like the looks of an' he turned awa' s' quickly, I think he was na wishin' t' be seen. It's a notion of mine he be followin' us."

"No, I have little money," I said. I thought back to the snake-eyed man from the upper Maine woods. "But it is a good thing to know."

Somebody had stood over me that night in the cabin. Somebody had wanted to search or kill me . . . and perhaps they still did. It was easy to imagine that they might want to steal and, likely destroy, Foulsham's papers. But, that was assuming my assailant knew of their existence and suspected that I had found him. Did they believe there was something else, something I knew, but must not live to tell?

Of course, there was Miss Majoribanks who also knew a good deal of this Baron Torville and his plotting, but she had only just joined us, or rather we had joined with her, afterward. The haunting thought returned. Either I had simply thwarted a thief who had hoped to steal from me as I slept and now found myself hopelessly suspicious or someone thought I might be connected with Foulsham to a greater extent than I was. Of course, I had been seen by Macklem carrying Foulsham's pistol, a pistol Macklem seemed to recognize.

Or was I imagining that too? Did Macklem have any connection with Foulsham at all? He was in the vicinity. I knew only that. He had been in the room when somebody made a move to either rob me or kill me, but I had no proof he was involved, or any real reason for suspicion.

Haverhill was just ahead, and we would be stopping there. I must be alert. We rode quietly along, but now I kept a closer eye on the trail behind and the brush along the way. We talked of many things for Macaire was a man who kept himself informed, and was keen in his judgments. And there was much to talk about. A man had just introduced the tin can into the United States, and was canning food. Daggett and Kensett were talking about using the process for canning fish in New York. Somebody wanted to introduce a bill that would permit Catholics to vote in Massachusetts, and Monroe was running for a second term.

The inn we found was a pleasant place, shaded by great old trees. We drew up in the shade and several men were sitting on a bench before the place . . . I knew none of them.

Miss Majoribanks adjusted her dress and dropped lightly down from the saddle.

"Will you take my horse, please?" she asked.

I did so.

"Please rub him down most carefully. And walk him a little before you put him in the stable." It was an order.

"I don't work for you, Miss Majoribanks."

"What? Who do you work for? I thought you were someone Macaire hired."

She knew better than that, but I simply said, "I work for no one. When I work it is as an independent contractor. If you ask me to care for your horse, as a favor, I should be pleased to so."

"As a *favor*? Of course not!" She turned sharply away. "Do not do it then. Macaire will handle it for me."

Her shoulders were very straight and I watched her go with pleasure at her beauty and with irritation at her manner. She seemed determined to think of me as a menial, and I refused the category. There was no work a menial might do that I would not willingly do myself . . . or had not done. It was her attitude that bothered me.

We put our own horses away, and Macaire was caring for the others. "Have you seen him again?" I asked him.

He shook his head. "No but we must be careful. The country is alive with thieves and highwaymen."

"We are a strong party," I commented, "it is not likely that we would be attacked."

Macaire considered the idea, and agreed. "You carry yourself well, with your rifle always handy. As fer the big man wi' you," he gave me a quick, thoughtful look, "he has the look of a pirate."

"Jambe-de-Bois? I think he is a man to leave alone."

"You do not know him?"

"We met on the road, and we travel the same way." I hesitated, but I trusted Macaire and liked him. "Sometimes I believe he knows more about me than he should.

I mean . . . well, perhaps when we met it was not altogether an accident."

Macaire gave me a thoughtful glance. "You are a shipwright, you say? Why, then? Why would any man be following a shipwright?"

I shrugged, and said nothing. Macaire worked carefully, grooming Miss Majoribanks' horse. I liked the way he worked, swiftly, easily, with no wasted motions. It was a thing I valued, for it was so I had been taught.

"John Daniel," Macaire said, "it is a good name, there is much going on here I do not understand."

"There is trouble afoot. You may be involved because of Miss Majoribanks' brother while I seem to have run across it by accident.

"En route south, I find a man who has been left for dead, attacked by that same Torville or someone allied to him. He was or had been a British officer, perhaps a British agent . . . now what was he doing on that lonely road through Maine when, by rights, his jurisdiction ended at the Canadian border? Was he following someone? Or was he, perhaps, en route to see your Miss Majoribanks?"

Macaire straightened up, staring at me, his motion ceased. "Now why would the mon be doin' that? We dinna ken the mon, nor he us."

"Charles Majoribanks wrote to his sister. He may have sent information elsewhere as well."

I was putting it all together as I spoke, and of course it was speculation, no more than that. Yet the coincidence would be great otherwise, and as much as coincidence interferes in all our lives, I did not like it.

Nor did Macaire. He went back to currying the horse, and I stood by, thinking as I watched him.

"One thing we know, Macaire," I suggested. "We are not alone on the road. One man has been killed, and I was attacked—"

He glanced up, and then I told him about the man who stood over me in the night at the inn.

"We must be careful," he said. "Very careful. I'd want no harm to come to the lady."

"Nor I," I said, and he looked at me, not too surprised, I think.

CHAPTER VIII

MORNING CAME WITH an uneasy sense of something impending, of something about to happen for which I was unprepared.

The common room of the inn was empty when I came down the steps from the room where I had slept. It was a warm, friendly room with a large table, several chairs and a fireplace upon which a small fire smoldered uneasily as if not sure whether it intended to burn or not. The floor looked washed and clean, and there were curtains at the windows. I went to the side of one window and peered out. The inn-yard was empty. It was hard-packed earth fringed by the green of new grass. There was nothing to allow for the feeling I carried, and when I straightened a voice said, "Lookin' for Injuns?"

Startled, I turned, having heard no sound.

The man was lean, taller than I, and somewhat stooped. What his age was I could not say, although I would have guessed him along in his late thirties. He might have been older. He wore buckskins, fringed, with a wide-brimmed hat, and moccasins on his feet. He, too, carried a rifle.

His gray eyes carried an amused look, but a friendly one. I grinned back at him. "You never can tell," I said. "An Indian might be any place."

He chuckled. "I reckon you'll do." He walked to the

fireplace and took up the blackened pot beside the coals. At a side-board he got down two cups. "Been here before," he said, "know my way around."

He filled the cups. "You the ones goin' west?"

Briefly, I hesitated. But I liked the man, liked his style and manner. "Yes," I said, "I'm going to Pittsburgh."

He frowned. "No further? Pittsburgh ain't anywhere. The frontier's moved west now. Pittsburgh an' Lexington . . . they was the places. Now y' got to go to St. Louis, on the Missouri."

"You know the Missouri?"

"I should smile. I been up it. Up the Platte, too."

His eyes took in the depth of my chest, the breadth of my shoulders. "You look fit for a mountain man."

"I'm a builder," I said, and then added, "I build boats. I want to build me a steamboat."

"Easier 'n walkin'," he agreed. "Keel-boat man, m'self. But mostly I favor horses." He sipped the black brew and looked up at me. "You the one travels with that peg-leg man?"

"We're goin' the same way, it seems. We're also travelling with Miss Majoribanks and Macaire."

His cup had started toward his lips, but now it stopped, hesitated, then continued the move. Something in what I said had stopped that cup, made him hesitate. I waited but he made no comment for several minutes. When I finished my coffee and threw the dregs into the coals he said, "Mind if I trail along?"

"You're going on west?"

"Yes, sir. Back to the beaver mountains. I want to trap the cricks that flow down from the high-up hills. I want to ride the Crow country, the Blackfoot country."

He had been squatting on his heels and now he got up. "Help you with your stock." He put down his cup. "You say you had a woman with you? A Miss—?"

"Majoribanks." I turned to look at him. "Do you know the name?"

He shrugged. "Now that there . . . unusual kinda name, ain't it? English, maybe?"

"Maybe . . . she's American though, old Yankee stock, and acts it."

He chuckled. "Heard she was right pert. Stiff-backed an' proud . . . well, that's the way a filly should be."

There might be two minds about that, I reflected, but we walked outside and then to the stable.

He moved easily, carrying his rifle like an extension of himself, and when we went to work on the stock, he knew what he was about. We put down more feed for them, saddled up, and loaded our gear on the pack horse. He brought his own gear and as our horse was carrying light, he added it to the pack. He had no horse himself.

"You'll not be able to keep up," I said.

He gave me a quick, hard glance. "You set your pace. I'll be along."

We led the horses out to the creek for water. It was a still, beautiful morning and the creek ran cheerfully along, shadowed by over-hanging trees. Morning sunlight sparkled on the water wherever it found its way through the leaves. The horses lifted their heads, water dripping from their muzzles. They seemed as pleased by the morning as we were.

We heard the hoof-beats as we turned from the water. A rider coming down the road at a comfortable pace. We led the horses back to the inn-yard as the rider appeared.

It was a woman, and she rode a fine bay gelding, and rode well.

She drew up as she entered the yard, her eyes going from me to my companion, then back to me. She was round-faced, pretty, probably on the sunny side of forty. "You must be that impudent young man," she said, staring at me, smiling a little.

"I'm not sure I could claim . . ." I trailed off because I wasn't really sure how to respond.

"Well, I am sure! No man could be so broad-shouldered without attracting attention. Yea, you'll be the one." She got down from the saddle without waiting for help.

"I am Mrs. Abigail Higgs. I shall be travelling west with you."

"That's a fine horse," I commented.

She addressed my companion. "You see? It has to be him. He meets a woman for the first time and comments on her horse. No wonder she thinks he's impudent." Abigail Higgs turned on me. "Are you impudent, young man?"

"Don't plan to be," I said.

She laughed. "I am for breaking my fast. Let's go in."

I tied her horse, glanced at the hunter and shrugged. He chuckled. "There's quite a woman. Be careful, young 'un."

Macaire was in the common room when we went in, and Jambe-de-Bois was coming down the stairs. Macaire glanced at my companion and I turned to introduce him, realizing for the first time that I had no idea as to his name.

"Mr. Macaire, meet—"

"Butlin," he said, "Calgary Butlin."

Macaire shook hands, measuring the hunter with shrewd, careful eyes. "Are you going west, mon?"

"I am."

"He'll be travelling with us." I hesitated, realizing I had spoken to no one of this, and so added, "With Jambe and me."

"He's welcome."

And then I added, "He's been up the Missouri, and is going back."

Macaire turned square around and looked at him again. "I would be speakin' t' you of that," he said shortly. "I have an interest westward."

"Alright . . . whenever you wish."

Butlin was an easy-moving man, light on his feet and graceful as a cat, which came from living in the woods and mountains. I'd done more than a bit of that myself. Jobs for a man with tools were often far apart, and I'd travelled by boat, canoe and foot through much of eastern Canada, building boats, bridges and barns.

I liked him. He was a wary, careful man who gave nothing in the way of advantage. When Abigail Higgs came down the road he had moved to the far side of his horse until he saw her plain, and when he sat down it was with his back to the wall where he could watch doors and windows. From the way he did it, it was easily seen as a matter of habit, not a sometime thing.

Abigail Higgs, who had been expected to join us at Haverhill, had gone up to Miss Majoribanks' room, so when they came downstairs to join us at the table Miss Majoribanks knew about Butlin. Nor did she waste any time.

"Mr. Butlin," she held out a hand, "I am Miss Majoribanks. You come from the western lands?"

"It has been two months," he said. "My brother was sick, but his body was buried before I could come to his side."

"I am sorry. Will you join our party?"

"I reckon I have, Miss. John Daniel here, he asked me."

She turned her eyes on me. "You presume too much! This is my party! I shall suggest who will join us!"

"Sorry," I said briefly, "I was not aware that I was of your party. We are only travelling in a similar direction. I feel free to invite whom I wish."

She turned her shoulder to me. "You *will* join us?" she said to Butlin.

"I reckon I have, Miss," he replied gently, "but if there's to be a split, I joined with him first."

Abruptly, she turned away and went to the table. Whatever else she had planned to ask him remained unasked, but I had an idea what the questions would be. Surely, in a country of so few white men a man named Majoribanks could not have gone unnoticed.

WE TOOK TO the road with the sun barely over the tops of the trees, but on this morning, it was I who led the way. I had my own reasons. There had been a brief shower in the night and I wanted a look at the road. Uneasiness was still upon me though there seemed no reason for it. I am not a man easily disturbed, and so felt there was a warning in the air.

Twice I drew up and studied the surface of the road.

Calgary Butlin came up beside me. "Early travellers," he commented, and I thought there was a somewhat ironic note in his voice.

"Before daylight, wouldn't you say?" I asked.

He walked his horse on a bit, studying the tracks. "Rained about an hour after midnight," he said, "this was after the rain. Maybe two, three o'clock. You were first down. You hear anything?"

Had I? I thought about that. Maybe it was the reason for the uncomfortable feeling I had.

"I don't think so," I said. "It was a mite after four when I rolled out, and day was breaking. There was light but no sun when I came down."

He nodded. "Something woke me. Might have been horses." He looked at the dust. "Two riders. Unlikely they would camp out so close to the inn, and unlikely they'd ride all night."

"You think somebody was scouting us?"

"Could be. There's thieves about."

We rode on for a few miles and then he suggested, "Can you get Macaire up here?"

He stopped and Macaire came up to us. Butlin explained about the tracks, and then he said, "I spent a summer hereabouts as a boy. There's a trace leads across country. An old Injun trail to Albany."

Macaire thought a moment. "Is it no so far?"

"Closer by miles."

"Alright."

The tracks went on along at a good pace, but Butlin suddenly turned and dipped into the trees at a point I'd not have guessed there'd be a trail, then he pointed it out to us, a dim narrow track leading off through the forest.

Macaire took the lead and Butlin dropped back and arranged the disturbed branches at our entry point, then brushed out our tracks and sifted leaves over them.

"They'll find it if they look," Butlin said, "but not unless they go back down the trail and track us to where we stepped off. We'll have us a good lead before they realize, I'm thinkin'."

It was a dim, shadowed place, and very still. We rode at a trot, then a walk, then a trot again. Twice we forded small streams.

By the time the sun was high, we were still within the forest, and we stopped briefly to spell the horses, gathering on the banks of a small pond, nobody talking.

The stillness was marvelous. Only a bird called from the branches nearby.

At mid-afternoon we crossed a wide meadow and came down into a country lane. Briskly then, we rode.

We skirted a small village and went back into the forest again. By sundown we had forty miles behind us and we stopped at a large, comfortable-looking farm. The women slept in the house, the rest of us outside in the barn. I awakened to the smell of fresh hay and the cackling of a hen who had just laid an egg and was informing the world.

A quick check of the trail showed no signs of travel and by an hour after sun-up we were dusting our tracks down the trail.

ALBANY WAS A small town that had once been Dutch. We came up to it over a plain dotted with pine along a very dusty road. The houses on the way to the town were few and poor. Albany had first been called Beverwyck, then changed to Fort Orange and after that to Williamstadt and finally Albany. Over the years there had been fires, like most frontier towns, but a few of the houses were still of the Dutch fashion with high, sharp roofs, small windows and low ceilings. Most of the streets were at right angles to the river, and there were some new, fine-looking houses. One that I noticed stood at the head of Market Street. It was said to be the house of a family named Van Rebnaselaer.

We ate a meal in the town, bought supplies, and rode out at once toward the west.

Now we followed no set route, but took bypaths and lanes or Indian trails, many long abandoned, across the country and generally down the course of the Allegheny River. We saw no night-time visitors, nor saw any travellers upon the trail before or behind, beyond the occasional country folk. Eventually, we rode into the town of Pittsburgh at the meeting of the rivers.

CHAPTER IX

MACAIRE DREW UP at a corner of Grant Street. He turned in his saddle. "You'll be stoppin' here?"

"I am. I'll be searching out a job of boat building here."

"Luck be with you. 'Tis a far piece we've come together and I'd wish it were all the way. You be good men and true," he said, "and I've slept easy these nights with the thought of you by."

Even Miss Majoribanks turned in her saddle, and I thought her features softened a little as she looked toward me. "I do not like saying goodbye," she said, "so I shall not."

"Nor I," I said quietly, "I do not envy you the trail you follow. Please be careful, for I think there are those who know why and where you go, and who want no one to see what they do."

"I shall manage," she replied coolly.

They turned aside then, riding toward Penn Street where Miss Majoribanks had friends with whom to stay. As for Jambe-de-Bois, Butlin and myself, we had no friends and no place to stay except what our money would buy.

Pittsburgh lay neatly between the Allegheny and the Monongahela rivers which joined at this point to form the Ohio. Fort Pitt, originally founded here many years before, had been a point of much warfare between Indians and whites, between French and English, and the site was important.

We found a hotel close by the river front and we stabled our horses nearby. It was the room for me, and a hot bath, but Jambe-de-Bois went along to the common room for a noggin of rum.

Calgary Butlin watched him go, and then said to me, "I shall go along the street. There be men from the mountains here."

We had not talked of what lay west, nor of Torville, so I said to him, "Say nothing, but if you hear a word of a man named Charles Majoribanks or of some plot brewing in the western lands, I'd like to know."

He gave me a thoughtful look and then said, "Let us go upstairs. There are things that need be said."

In my room he sat in a window seat, cross-legged as he preferred to sit. "This man, he is related to the young lady?"

"Brother," I said. "She is going west to find him. She believes he is in some kind of trouble."

"He may have crossed the trail of some rather dangerous men," Butlin said wryly.

"What do you know of all this?"

"There are no secrets in the west, although there are some who believe otherwise. No man moves but what someone sees, and no man speaks but what someone listens. Indians are curious folk, and often puzzled by the things done by white men. They discuss them over their pipes.

"There are men among the Indians who talk of war. There is talk of guns, of many rifles that will come from the sea. Men move from tribe to tribe along with some disgruntled Indians, and it is said that many of the Indians listen with both ears."

IT WAS DARK when I again went out to the street. There was a gleam of reflected light on the waters of the Monongahela, and I stood there for a few minutes, just looking at the river and listening.

From up the street came the tinny sound of a piano, and somebody whooped. Two men passed me, smelling of wine and tar, both a little unsteady. I walked toward the river. From somewhere close by I could smell the good smell of fresh lumber, and then I saw it, great tiers of planks stacked to season in the sun, and a cribbing of heavy timbers and poles for masts.

My thoughts returned to Miss Majoribanks and her voyage to the west. Uneasily, I recalled my promise to Simon Tate . . . yet the promise had only been to see her safely here. Now she was going to St. Louis, and if she found no word of her brother, she would go up the Missouri or the Platte.

Macaire was a good man, a solid man. I tried to convince myself not to worry.

Yet I did worry. She was too young, too sure of herself. I walked on along the waterfront, seeing several keel-boats and at least one hull that appeared from its shallowness to be that of a steamboat being built for service on the Missouri.

There was a light in a shack near the farthest stacks of lumber. Beyond it the bank sloped away and I could see flat-boats moored along the river. From some of them came a sound of voices, and the cabins showed light from the windows. Men lived on these boats while they floated down river to New Orleans, on arrival they sold the boats and their contents and paid passage back up-stream.

Then I saw it. I stopped, caught in mid-stride, straining my eyes in the dim light. It was a monster; a dragon-headed monster with the body of a serpent, rearing up from the river and carrying a steamboat on its back. I approached the dock.

It was the *Western Engineer*—the boat that had gone west with the Major Stephen H. Long expedition. Even in Canada, news of the expedition had been heard. Thirty-five days from Pittsburgh to St. Louis with several stops along the way. From there she went west on what had been intended to be a voyage of discovery and exploration. I looked at the shape of the hull and the strange snake-like cladding incorporated into the design, its head reared above the waterline, its tail fins covering the view of the stern paddle wheel from the sides.

It was something to see, even in the darkness as I walked along the dock. It had been built, they said, to frighten the Indians. I'd known a few Indians and I doubted whether any of them would be frightened for long. Yet from a distance the thing must have been impressive, steaming along up-stream against the current, smoke issuing from its nostrils, water foaming behind it.

"Like her?"

A man was leaning on the rail right above the scaly back.

"She must have been a joy to build."

"Build? Aye . . . I'd no hand in that, but she takes the river nicely. I'd say it's a shame."

"Shame?"

"She's government built, and the government has had their fill of her. They're takin' her up the Ohio a ways and she'll be junked."

A glance at her hull . . . she'd be about seventy-five feet long. "How much does she draw?"

"Nineteen inches. She's right for the western rivers where often enough you have to chase the water to find it."

"How about her boilers?"

"No trouble. She's a good craft . . . but small for the southern rivers and there's little market yet in the west. It's simply that she was sent to do a job, and it was only half-done, but that was the fault of the men aboard and the difficulties that arose."

We talked a bit longer, and I am afraid my questions were more about conditions up river than the possibilities of work. The trouble was, I was beginning to feel the fever.

When a man came into Pittsburgh, Cincinnati or Lexington in those days he found himself meeting folks from all over who talked of only one thing: the west. Everybody either had been west or was going there. They talked of Indians, buffalo, beaver, and more than anything else they talked about the land, the endless prairies and the high mountains.

Sometimes it made no sense. I mean men with good jobs, professions or businesses, were talking of going west. Many of them had only to stay where they were to get rich, but there was a drive in them that went beyond money, beyond success. It was the drive to explore, to develop new country, to escape a world where civilization defined them.

It was in the air a man breathed in those frontier towns, and must be even more so out there in St. Louis where everybody was determined to go. There was talk of opening trade with Santa Fe, and talk of California, wherever that was.

This man had the fever too. His name was John Massman, and he had been to St. Louis twice before and up the Missouri with a keel-boat before that.

"Injuns? I've known a-plenty. Good folks, but notional. They can change their minds in a minute, and they think lightly of the white man. Most of them have seen few of us and we all want to trade.

"The Injun is convinced the white man can't get along without him. Buffalo robes are all important to an Injun, and he believes the white man has no buffalo to hunt so he has to come west to get robes from the Injun.

"A few Injuns have been east and seen the cities, but the other Injuns don't believe what they say. They call them liars, and say the white man's medicine has confused them.

"You got to walk soft until you know how the wind blows . . . if'n you do business with one tribe another's liable to take you for an enemy. Some tribes will steal you blind, others can be trusted with your life . . . you got to walk easy until you know where they stand."

After talking with Massman for some time I walked back to the hotel. Jambe-de-Bois was sitting in the common room combing his beard and muttering. He combed his beard when he got worried, and he was worried now.

He had a glass of rum before him and from his flushed cheeks, I knew it was not the first, although he was a man who drank little and could hold his liquor.

"They're here, lad," he said to me. "They've come up to us."

"Who?"

"Macklem and that lot. Only there's more of them now. And a rum lot they are, too! They've tied in with eight or ten rascals from God knows where and they're fixing to go west."

"It is none of our affair," I said, shrugging. "The sooner they go the better."

He shot me a hard glance, eyes bulging a bit as they were likely to do when he was over-wrought. "None of our affair, you say? That may be one way of thinking, but I think we're lashed to them, sink or swim, until someone drowns!"

He took a short swallow of rum. "That one with the sneaky eyes . . . he was in here, askin' after you. He didn't see me," he indicated the rear, "I was back yonder by the door, and he asked partic'lar for you."

"All right, he knows where I am."

"And that wasn't all." Jambe-de-Bois wiped his beard with the back of his hand. "He asked after the young miss."

There was a sudden stillness in me. Jambe had all my attention, and he knew it.

"He asked for her?"

"He did. But nobody knew aught of her here, and he

went away after a quick look around him. Oh, he's a suspicious lot, that one!"

Abruptly, I dropped into a chair across from him. How much they inquired after me did not matter. I could take care of myself, or try. With Miss Majoribanks it was a different thing. She was a fine, proud young lady with no idea what she was getting into, nor would she let Macaire tell her. As for her other young friend, he didn't seem like he could tell her nor would if he could.

She was going west to look for her brother who had discovered, or thought he had, some kind of plot. I did not doubt there might be some such plan, for there had been many such. The Louisiana Territory, in particular, seemed to attract political schemers. There had been a range of them from George Rogers Clark and Edmond Genet to Aaron Burr and Harman Blennerhassett.

These plots were well known in my country, for men from the Gaspe had talked about what they meant for French America, and even of becoming involved. The very existence of such a vast, unexplored area was a temptation to every adventurer or soldier-of-fortune, and each one dreamed of becoming a king overnight, a king of his own vast land, vaguely reported to be as large as Europe.

The success of the Lewis and Clark expedition had only added fuel to their dreams, for if sixteen men or so could travel across a continent, couldn't a few hundred men, perhaps allied with some Indians, like Cortez or Pizarro, seize it for themselves?

The real question, however, was what was happening *now*?

If Miss Majoribanks could be believed, her brother,

Charles, had somehow become involved in or aware of a plot whose seriousness I was not qualified to judge. Not long after, I had come upon the body of a dying man, a British agent, who was somehow involved in that very plot. The, so-called, Colonel Macklem had been stopping at the next inn, and with him a bunch of men who, if not rascals, at least looked the part. That same Macklem had proved himself an exceptionally dangerous man by his killing of Sam Purdy.

Now Macklem was here in Pittsburgh inquiring about, or having one of his henchmen inquire about, Miss Majoribanks. It was true that I had warned her, but she seemed to take my warning very casually.

Lastly, rumor had it that many rootless men, adventurers and rogues, were drifting west led by stories of a plot to seize Louisiana. If this was so then Macklem and his group might well be such a band, and they might already know of the activities of her brother on the frontier.

All of this was intriguing, but what business was it of mine? This was not my country. I was a Canadian.

Yet, somehow I found that a feeble excuse. Many of us were living and working on the American side of the border and no doubt as many Americans were on the Canadian side, and nobody cared. Our countries had too many things in common and our problems were too similar. The border was a technicality, a line for politicians to argue over. As long as we supported common values it wasn't a boundary of morality or good citizenship. Did that mean I was obligated to act in the defense of the United States? It was all too complicated.

"That's none of my affair," I grumbled. "She has been warned."

"Hah!" Jambe-de-Bois said explosively. "Warned! Did you ever know such a high-headed young filly to take to a warning?"

"Well, that's up to her."

"Is it? It was in my mind that you were having ideas about her. Not that I'd blame you, lad, she's right pretty, that one, right pretty!"

I tossed off my bit of rum. He was right, but she had shown little respect for my attentions. "I am for sleep," I grumbled. "Let her go her way."

Getting to my feet, I added, "Anyway, she has Macaire."

"Macaire! Do you think he's a match for that lot? Macaire's a solid man, a good man, but he's not up to Macklem's boot tops. Macklem would swallow him whole then spit him out."

"I work with timber," I said stubbornly. "I came to build boats."

"Aye . . . so the girl can go to the devil."

"Who are you to talk so to me? You're a damned pirate!"

He laughed, baring his ugly teeth in the process. "Pirate, is it? *You* say that to me? Your own pirate blood runs thick in your veins. Do you think I bought that John Daniel story? You've the mark of the Talon upon you, and if you had a claw for a hand you'd be the spittin' image of the old devil himself!"

Well! I stared at him. Who was this man who had come out of the night and the swamp and who knew me by name?

We were almost alone in the room, and our voices had been low but intense. Several had turned their eyes upon us, seeking the beginning of a quarrel, or so they thought.

"If my name be Talon, I said, so be it, Jean Daniel Talon, if you wish to know, and it is said the old man of my tribe was a pirate. What is that to you?"

He had half-risen from his chair, now he sat down. "Sit, damn you, and we'll talk. You called me a pirate, and I have been that, and more. No better gunner ever sailed the seas than I, and sometimes I sailed under the black flag, but that be neither here nor there.

"Do you think those who sailed the Indian seas have forgotten the Old Claw? They remember him. Believe me, they do, and how he took the fortress of Gingee, single-handed."

"He did not take it. He merely entered it."

"Entered it," he says. "Yes, he entered it, entered it when no army could have done so, scaled walls and towers right into the inner rooms and bearded the old lion in his den, then killed him and carried off a bag of loot that would ransom half the kings of Europe! Who in those waters does not know the story?

"Aye, and I've looked upon the walls of Gingee these many years after, and I shudder to think of a man who would dare them alone."

A figure loomed over the table. Glancing up, startled, I saw it was the man from the steamboat, John Massman. "Maybe I shall join you in building, for I am out of a job. They've sold the boat."

"The *Western Engineer*?"

"Aye . . . sold it to a bit of a lass named Majorbank or some such name."

Something sank within me. "To Miss Majoribanks?"

"That's her." He was sour with the taste of it. "I wanted another trip aboard her . . . she's a good boat . . . but her captain said no. He had his own crew."

"Her captain?"

"Aye, she wastes no time, that girl. She bought the boat and found a crew in no time at all. She hopes to have stores and fuel aboard and be gone within hours, and if I know men, that Macklem will have it done. He looks a slave driver to me."

"Macklem?"

"Aye. *Captain* Macklem now, with sailing orders for St. Louis and points west."

Massman sat down.

My eyes turned to Jambe-de-Bois. There was no triumph in him, no I-told-you-so, there was just disappointment . . . and fear.

Miss Majoribanks was going west on the *Western Engineer* with Macklem for captain, going to the rescue of a brother who might well be a prisoner of the same bad lot who crewed her vessel!

CHAPTER X

JAMBE-DE-BOIS SHOOK his head slowly. He was scowling. "Too late now. Macklem is a charmer. If he's talked to her you'd get no place arguing against him. In fact, if you tried it he would be all smiles and friendly, and when you got out of her sight, he'd kill you."

"Maybe I am not easy to kill."

He waved a hand. "That was what Sam Purdy thought, and Macklem destroyed him."

"I shall call upon her."

"You'll do no good. She's found a man who will take her where she wants to go, he listens to her, and he tells her she is right that she can go west. He needed a way, and now she's made it easy for him, and his crew. You cross them and they'll kill you."

"Nevertheless, I shall go to see her."

He glanced at the clock in the tavern. "It is after midnight. You cannot go now."

"In the morning, then."

Needless to say, I slept not at all that night, and was up with the first light. I say I slept none, yet certainly I must have, in snatches here and there. With the first crack of dawn I was having coffee and without waiting for breakfast I went out upon the street.

Two men leaned against the hitching rail. One was a man with a stocking-cap on and a gold ring in his ear.

The other wore a black slouch hat, and both were husky, capable-looking men. Yet I merely noted them and turned toward town.

As I did so, one of them called out. "Wrong way, Mister. If you're huntin' work, go the other way, toward the boat-docks."

"Thanks. I have business uptown."

They were walking toward me, spreading out a little as they came. "You better go to the boat-docks. Nobody wants to see you uptown. Fact is, we was warned most particular that you shouldn't go uptown."

I smiled pleasantly. "I suppose you'd stop me if I tried to go?"

The man with the stocking-cap grinned. "Why, now. We wouldn't wish for you to get into trouble, would we, Pete?"

"We surely wouldn't," Pete said. "He might have notions of callin' on a certain young lady. Wouldn't do, no way."

"Well," I said. "I suppose you're right. I might as well go back and eat breakfast."

"There! I told you he was smart, Pete! Didn't I tell you? I just said to you, 'That boy's smart. He wanted to be told no second time,' an' what did you say?"

"I said we should teach him a little lesson. Sort of impress him."

My three steps had taken me close to them. I put my right hand up to hitch my collar into better position, and I threw the punch from there. Now I was always taught to punch *through* what I was hitting at, as if my target was at the back of the head instead of the chin.

I threw that right high and across and without losing

momentum I just let my natural shoulder swing carry me and came back with a left that caught Mr. Stocking-cap coming in. I'd have been surprised if either of them got up, and I was not surprised. Feeling suddenly cheerful I turned and went uptown.

Penn Street had a row of elegant houses, but I'd not come unprepared. Before coming out on the street I had put on my tailored black suit. It was one I'd had made in Montreal on my last visit and it was beautifully styled.

The house toward which I'd been directed was a fine-looking mansion, and the black woman who opened the door bowed me in when I asked for Miss Majoribanks.

"Oh?" she looked surprised when she saw me. I don't know whether it was just me or the handsome black suit. "Oh, Mr. Daniel! This is . . . unexpected."

A very pretty blonde young lady came through the door behind her. Miss Majoribanks turned and said, "Helen, excuse me. This is Mr. Daniel. He was with us when we came down from Maine."

"How do you do?" Helen had big blue eyes, which she widened very effectively as she took my hand. "We are just sitting down to breakfast; won't you join us?" She turned. "Daisy, put another place on for Mr. Daniel."

I followed them through to a handsome room with walnut panels and upholstered furniture. The table set better than any I'd seen since my grandfather's place.

"Helen?" Miss Majoribanks' features were stiff. "I am afraid you misunderstand. Mr. Daniel is . . . is . . . I mean he's not . . . ?"

"A gentleman?" I suggested. "Isn't that a matter of

opinion, Miss Majoribanks? And have you ever found me to be otherwise?"

Her cheeks were flushed. Obviously embarrassed, she said, "I mean . . . I did not *invite* you here. This is the home of a friend; I cannot presume to—"

"Invite a laborer? A man who works with his hands?"

I held out my hands to Helen. "Are they so bad? These hands?" I smiled at her. "Is it so bad to shape wood, to build?"

She took my hands, laughing. "Why! They're wonderful hands. And so *strong*-looking! They make me shiver!"

Miss Majoribanks' lips tightened a little. I had a feeling that some sort of skirmish was developing but, regardless of what it was all about, I was being given food and the opportunity to make my case.

Helen held my right hand by the fingers and led me to the table. "Sit here! Please do! Daisy, Mr. Daniel is a big a man and I am sure he's very hungry."

It was a pleasure to sit at such a table again, though despite its richness it lacked a little something one might have found at my grandfather's home.

"Are you staying in Pittsburgh long, Mr. Daniel?"

"That depends." The coffee was strong and hot. "I came here hoping to build boats. Perhaps to build one for myself, for trade on the western waters, but certain matters have come up . . . that's the reason I came here this morning. I had to speak to Miss Majoribanks."

"To Tabitha?"

It was the first time I had heard her name . . . Tabitha Majoribanks . . . I couldn't decide whether I liked it or not.

"Is it personal? Must I leave?"

"No . . . it's business." I put down my cup. "Miss Majoribanks, if you will permit me. I understand you have bought the steamboat *Western Engineer*?"

"Yes, I have. It was going for a very reasonable price and it seemed much the simplest and easiest way to go west."

"I'm sure it is. You have a crew?"

"Of course. Colonel . . . I mean Captain Macklem has taken care of all that. He's very efficient."

"And so handsome!" Helen exclaimed.

I paused, not sure how to proceed. Tabitha Majoribanks looked at me expectantly. "This Colonel Macklem," I said, "is the man who killed Sam Purdy."

"The Mr. Purdy who attacked him?"

"No doubt. I was thinking of the manner of it. Also, he was on the road in Maine when Foulsham was killed, the British officer."

Tabitha Majoribanks knew where the conversation was going now, and her eyes were chilly. "And you, Mr. Daniel? Were you not on that road also?"

"Yes, I was. But Foulsham was alive when I found him."

"And did he accuse Colonel Macklem?" Her tone was cold.

"No, but—"

She stood up. "Mr. Daniel, I have no idea what you hoped to gain by coming here, nor what you wish me to believe, but if you are jealous of—"

"Jealous?" I remained seated. "And why should I be jealous? What reason could I possibly have?"

Her cheeks flushed, and her eyes narrowed to pinpoints. She had a fine sort of anger, this Tabitha Majoribanks! It made her remarkably handsome, too. Beautiful was not quite the word at the moment.

I got up then and before she could speak, I said quietly, "You believe your brother has come upon something important to your country. And Mr. Foulsham, Captain Foulsham, was pursuing a man, or at least investigating one, who had betrayed *his* country, a notorious adventurer.

"By your own admission a certain Baron Torville is now recruiting all the riffraff he can find with a view, you said, to seizing the Territory. Well, Colonel Macklem, with a considerable group of riffraff, are now going aboard your steamer. If your boat is the easiest way to the western lands for you, it is so for him . . . for them."

"You are accusing him?" Her eyes were coldly furious.

"No. I have not sufficient evidence. What I am suggesting is that you find another crew. Find one known to the local people, and a captain known as well."

"You have not sufficient evidence. I should think not. All you have is your imagination and your dislike for Mr. Macklem. I am sorry, Helen, but I can no longer remain in the room with this man."

"I am leaving." I turned to Helen. "I'm sorry. I had information and I hoped she would listen, but I did not mean to disrupt your breakfast."

She walked to the door with me. "You will come again, won't you? And please . . . don't take offense. I have never seen her so angry before. She must like you a great deal."

"*Like* me? *Her?* She detests the ground I walk on."

She giggled. "I doubt it. It was what you said about no

reason for jealousy that really burned. Do come again, Mr. Daniel."

"Call me Jean," I said, "that's really my name."

IT WAS SEVERAL blocks before I could find a crossing that was not too muddy, and I walked slowly, turning the whole affair over in my mind.

My efforts had been useless. Now she was angry, and if I was any judge of people the last thing she would think of doing would be to rid herself of Macklem. I had really made things worse, for all my good intentions.

Macaire . . . I must warn Macaire.

Suddenly I was alert. I must move with care. Those two men who awaited me outside had not been there by accident, but obviously to prevent me from doing just what I had done . . . only I'd made a proper mess of it.

Macklem . . . or somebody close to him, for whom he was acting . . . certainly believed that I knew more than I did. No doubt he suspected I could go to them with concrete information, and wished to prevent that.

Butlin was loafing on Water Street, obviously watching for me. He sauntered my way. "Looks like you had trouble," he said.

"No trouble," I said.

"But a feller at the inn said you was jumped by two toughs."

"Oh, that." I grinned at him. "That was nothing compared to what I ran into when I tried to warn Miss Majoribanks about Macklem."

Briefly, I explained. Butlin stood quiet, listening. He was a good listener, Butlin was, and a man who remembered. Above all, as I was learning, he was a man who knew how to act on what he had learned. Many men have information, but few know how to use it to advantage.

"So, what do we do now? Jambe-de-Bois is worried."

"I want to talk to Macaire. Find him for me, will you? I shall change clothes."

My room was quiet. The hotel had emptied of many of the overnight guests, and even the common room was empty. From my window I could see the *Western Engineer* down at the river bank. From my pack-back I got out my spy glass and studied the steamboat.

A man was standing on a skiff painting out the ship's name. Several men were walking up the gangway carrying boxes and bales. Macklem was wasting no time.

A wagon drawn by two horses had drawn up near the gangway. The back of the wagon was covered with a tarpaulin, and as I watched several men appeared to surround the wagon, all were facing out. Six husky men came down the gangway and the back of the tarpaulin was lifted and a long box taken out, then another and another.

As I watched, I counted. There were at least ten of those long boxes, and nobody needed to tell me what they contained, for I had seen such before. Each box contained at least a dozen rifles . . . perhaps more.

There was a light tap on the door, and Butlin came in. Handing him the glass, I indicated the wagon, now drawing away. Another was just pulling up, and it was unloaded in the same way.

"Well?" I said.

He glanced at me. "Rifles?"

"Of course. There must have been at least a hundred on that first wagon."

"So we can guess, a modest estimate, no less than two hundred rifles aboard, and probably more. That's a lot of firepower."

"You've been up the Missouri, Butlin. How far up?"

He hesitated, then slowly lowered the glass again. "As far as you can go, an' I wasn't the first, either. You ever hear of Jeremy Pinch? Or Captain Zachary Perch?"

"No."

"Well, neither has anybody else, but they were up there, right around the head of the Missouri an' maybe out to the Columbia as early as 1807 . . . maybe earlier."

"Who were they?"

"You make your guess, I'll make mine. They were supposed to be part of a government expedition."

"Did you ever hear of David Thompson?"

"Met him one time . . . away off up to the north. He explored more country than Lewis and Clark, saw most of Canada before any other white man . . . at least, he was among the first."

"My father knew him. He was to do some scouting around for my father down below the mouth of the Columbia, but when he got there, Astor had moved in so he had no chance."

We were silent. The second wagon had discharged its cargo and moved away. Now there was only the usual activity around the hull of the dragon boat.

"What are you going to do?" Butlin asked.

There was nothing I could do. Tabitha Majoribanks would not have me aboard, and I certainly would not serve under Macklem. "Nothing," I said, "but hunt a job."

Butlin dropped into a chair and stared thoughtfully out the window. "That's a fine girl," he muttered, "a fine, proud girl."

Something inside me cringed. I felt a shame come over me. Yes, she was all of that. I remembered the set of her shoulders and the look of her back as she walked away from me . . . but I knew she had no use for me, and although she was a fine, proud girl she also had a devil of a temper and an arrogance there seemed to be no saving her from.

I said as much. Butlin chuckled. "Would you have it otherwise? If you're going to have steam in the kettle you've got to have fire in the stove."

A man was walking up the gangway, pausing at the rail. It was Colonel Macklem, and something in me made my fists clench.

But no . . . that was not the right approach. If a man was to tackle Macklem, he must do it with a calm mind and a steady hand, for that one was thinking. He was thinking all the time.

And every thought was of how to kill you, how to make you suffer.

CHAPTER XI

AT THE BOAT-YARD I had no trouble. Keel-boats were in demand and men were needed. The timbers were cut in a saw-mill but many needed added shaping, and I was better than a fair hand with ax or adze.

On the afternoon of my first day, John Dill walked over to where I was working and kicked the chips I'd cut from a timber, in facing it. The chips were almost uniform in size, and the timber as smooth as if polished.

"You're good," he said quietly. "Have you built boats?"

"I am a shipwright," I told him. "I have built three schooners, a barkentine and several brigs, along with a number of fishing craft."

"I thought so." He watched me work for a time. "Have you built bridges?"

"Several . . . and barns, as well."

"We've a steamer to build. One hundred and twenty-five feet overall, main deck, cabin-deck and a texas."

I leaned on my ax. "You will build it here?"

"I shall . . . if you'll have the job, it is yours."

"You mean I shall be in charge?"

"I've watched you work. You'll do it. I want the job done by a man who loves his work, who loves the wood he works with and the tools he uses."

It was what I wanted. It was what I had come west to

do, and now it was here. One hundred and twenty-five feet would make a handsome craft, and once I'd put one in the water I could write my own ticket.

Why did I hesitate?

"Mr. Dill? Let me give you my answer tomorrow. I must think of what must be done, and what I have to do."

"Well enough. I've an office yonder at the end of Water Street. Anybody can tell you. Come along when you've made up your mind."

For a moment longer I waited, thinking, and then once more I went to work, liking the clean, neat strokes of the adze, the way the chips broke away. This was what I had started to do in life, to build, to build boats that would carry the commerce of this wild land, go up its farthest rivers.

When I finished my day it was dark. I stacked my tools and turned away from the river toward the hotel. If I was going to remain here and work I must find new, less expensive quarters.

There was a faint scuff of feet upon the street ahead of me. I stood very still. There had been that bit of trouble on the previous day, but I hoped for no more.

Ready for trouble, I stepped up to the walk.

"John Daniel?" It was Macaire.

"Aye. What can I do for you, sir?"

"You can sail with us. You can come in any capacity you like . . . or as a passenger, or a free-trader."

"You speak for yourself, Macaire. Neither Macklem nor Miss Majoribanks would allow it."

"If I speak for you, they'll take you. Will y' come, lad?"

"I cannot. Your Miss Majoribanks thinks I am common stuff, and dislikes me into the bargain. As for Macklem, we'd kill each other within the week."

"Ah, y' dinna know him, lad. That's a canny one, yon, smooth as a French tailor. He'd say naught against you. In fact, an' this will surprise y' lad, he suggested it."

"*Macklem* did?"

"Aye, your name was up, I dinna know if it were she who mentioned it, or whether it was he himself, but your name was up. She said you'd been companions on the way down, and he come out with it, quick and easy. Have him aboard," he says, "in any capacity he wishes."

I considered that. Now why have me aboard? Obviously, to be watched, and then done away with when the chance offered.

"No," I said, "I will not come, Macaire. You're a good man, and I would stand beside you in this trouble, for there's trouble a-coming whether she believes it or not."

We were walking alone on the street toward the hotel, and he said, "You know too little of the lass, John Daniel. She kens what's ahead, better than any of us."

"She does?"

"Lad, her father was a canny mon. He had those who knew writing to him from all about. The lass knows more than the both of us. Do not underrate her. She's got a good head on the pretty shoulders of hers, a canny head. She's like her pa . . . only more, lad, more."

We walked the rest of the way in silence. At the tavern door, I said, "Come in for a drink."

"No. I should be at her side."

He left me there and I walked inside and went aloft to

my room under the eaves. When I lit the candle, Butlin was there, resting easy in my chair.

"How did it go, then?" he asked.

"Well enough." And then I told him of the chance to build the steamboat.

"From John Dill himself, is it? Aye, he's a knowing man. He's been up the Mississippi, and he's sailed on the lakes, and helped to build the first horse-boat there . . . you know the kind where the paddle wheels are turned by horse-power?"

"Aye?"

"He helped to build the *Accommodation,* some ten years back, at Montreal. He worked on the *Swiftsure,* and tried to buy a piece of the *Walk-In-The-Water* before building began. He knows boats, and he believes in steam."

The names were familiar to me. All were Great Lakes steamers, and there'd been a time when I thought of going down to Sackett's Harbor to work on the American steamer *Ontario*.

"Well," he said at last, "you have what you wanted. It is surely your chance, and with a good man, a solid man. If you do this one well you'll have a future, lad, for he has the name of seeking out good men and keeping them by him."

I told him about Macaire, and what he had said of Miss Majoribanks. Butlin did not seem surprised, and I said as much.

"Talon," he said, "I have known of Miss Majoribanks for more than two years, and Macaire is right. There's no shrewder person in the country than she."

"But she's just a girl!"

He chuckled. "Oh, sure! That's all she is, a girl. But she has a head on her shoulders that is older and wiser than many a man twice her age. You forget she grew up at her father's knee, helping with the business, often making decisions, handling the writing. Believe me, her pen is known to a hundred men west of here, and they'd die for her.

"I doubt any of us could tell her little about Torville that she does not know. Her father was reputed to have files on them all, you know, the filibusterers and adventurers; Burr, Wilkinson, Murrell, Genet, the explorations of David Thompson's. Believe me, lad. Thompson was one of the greatest, a man too little-known for what he's done. But you said your father knew him?"

"Aye. Before he ever went west, and they exchanged letters after. His name was one mentioned about our table at home."

Peeling off my shirt, I bathed in the basin, dumped the water out of the window and filled the basin again from the white pitcher. It was cold, but it felt good on my arms and chest. When I had dried off, I put on a fresh shirt and we went down to the common room below.

WHEN WE WERE seated at a table I said, "If we do the steamer, I'll be needing help. Will you work with me?"

"Thanks . . . but no. I may go to look after the lass."

"Miss Majoribanks?" I could not call her Tabitha.

"She will need help. She knows what it is she faces, but she will not quit. She will find her brother, alive or dead, and if dead she'll find where the body lies. You can be sure of it."

I shifted uneasily. The food was being put before us, but suddenly I was not so hungry.

"What are you to her?" I asked.

"I am nothing. Only I was one of those to whom she wrote a time or two, and to whom she once sent help in time of need." He placed his hands on the table, staring at the meat before him. "She knows me not, for names have a way of changing."

"Few names remain the same over the years. Most have changed."

"Mine was Boutevillaine. The name was put on articles and mis-spelled Butlin, so I let it stand. It is simpler that way."

"A name is what a man makes it," I said, "but I'll be sorry not to have you with me."

"Aye . . . and I'd be better off to stay, for I've a thought 'twill be bad to the westward, with Indians and all. But she will need help. She has only Macaire and the other one . . . and he's not worth much."

He left, and I felt relieved that he was going with them. I trusted none of that lot save Macaire, and was sure that for all her information that she was putting her head in the lion's mouth. Yet, with me, she had barely been polite and it was no affair of mine.

Suddenly I recalled that it had been some time since I had seen Jambe-de-Bois. As a matter of fact, I had seen nothing of him since the morning when I left to call on Miss Majoribanks.

When I had eaten, I inquired of the inn-keeper about Jambe-de-Bois, but he had seen nothing of him, so I went back upstairs to my room.

Glancing from the window I saw there were lights on

the deck of the steamer, and some work was going on. Watching for a few minutes I could make out nothing but occasional movement along the deck. The wharf was shrouded in darkness.

Undressing, I got into bed, clasped my hands behind my head and considered the building of the steamboat, and the problems it would entail. Yet through the thoughts of building, costs, time, and materials, her face kept appearing, laughing, angry, contemptuous, cool . . . but always her face.

Disgusted, I sat up. What was the matter with me? Why should my thoughts continually revert to *her*?

Then, barely audible in the quiet of the night, there was a tap on my door, the faintest tap, almost as if it wished not to be heard.

CHAPTER XII

MY HAND REACHED for the pistol that lay upon the table. A moment of listening, and the tap came once again.

It was very late. Sliding quickly from bed, I drew on my pants and tucking the gun behind my belt, I stepped to the door.

"Who is it?" I asked.

"Macklem," a voice answered.

Right hand upon my gun, I opened the door with my left and took a quick step back, drawing the gun as I did so.

Macklem stood there, filling the door.

He stepped on into the room, and I knew from his manner that his eyes had swept it corner to corner to see if we were alone. He noticed the pistol, and chuckled. "Afraid?" he said.

"Careful," I replied quietly, "just careful."

"You have talked to Miss Majoribanks," he said, "and I gather there was some disagreement."

"Of a sort," I said, committing myself to nothing. He drew back a chair and sat down. "Can we have a light?"

"The candle is there," I pointed with the muzzle of the gun, "if you wish it lit, by all means, light it."

He did so. The match flared briefly, the wick caught; the flame lifted up.

"You do not trust me," he said, as if sorrowed by the fact.

I chuckled. "Not even a bit."

He waved a hand. "No matter. Regardless of that, we need you."

" 'We'?"

"All of us. Miss Majoribanks, Macaire, and I. We are going west, into unknown country, into Indian country. Macaire says that you understand travel in rough country, that you have dealt with Indians. I've come to ask you to join us.

"Besides," he added, "Miss Majoribanks would feel safer if you were along."

"Did she say that?"

"No," he admitted, "but I sense it. Whether you know it or not, she believes in you. She trusts you."

"Hah!" I grunted.

"I do not joke. We have far to go, and beyond St. Louis, who knows what awaits us?"

"I'm sorry," I said. "I have an excellent offer to build a steamboat here. It is what I came west to do."

He was silent for a few moments. "You are a Canadian?" he asked suddenly. "From Quebec?"

"I am."

He hesitated again, as if uncertain as to how to proceed. I was quite sure that he did want me along, for many an accident can happen on such a trip and I did not believe he wanted to leave any loose ends lying about. He did not know how much I knew, but suspected I knew too much. Of this I was sure.

"We need a man of your skills," he said. "On such a trip, there is much danger and often a need for repairs.

Miss Majoribanks wishes to go up some of the unknown rivers, and there will be no boat-yards there, nor any skilled workmen."

"I would have thought," I said coolly, "that among the men you have with you there would be various skills. I am sure you will manage."

"There's also the matter of companionship," he suggested. "You are obviously a man of intelligence, of breeding."

"What do you know of my class?"

He waved a hand. "It is obvious. You are a gentleman, a man of culture and background. It is in your bearing, your style, your manner of speech. You are most certainly of French ancestry, but not completely so."

"Not completely no," I agreed. "And you, Colonel Macklem? What is your ancestry? Your breeding? I do not find it so obvious."

He looked up at that, and the glance he shot at me was not pleasant. I had touched a nerve, a point of extreme sensitivity. It was a thing to remember.

"Does it matter?" He stood up suddenly, so suddenly that I took an involuntary step backward. It irritated me, for he noticed and was amused. "What matters is that we must have you with us. What inducement can I offer? A chance to trade for furs? To look for gold? To become suddenly rich in some other way? You seem to be a fighting man—"

"I?"

"You." He looked across the table at me. "We understand each other, you and I.

"We are men of the world. To the west there are vast lands, free for the taking. There are estates to be had vaster than anything of which the feudal lords of Europe could dream. To build a boat is all very well, but to own a thousand square miles . . . every inch of it yours . . . that is something! Fortunes await the strong, and the land is there for the taking."

"What of the Indians?"

"Those whom we call Indians were not always here. They pushed others out when they came. It is the way of the world, with animals and plants as well as men, and those most fitted to survive will survive.

"Even now they are continually raiding one another. Some tribes have been compelled to join others for protection when too many of their own warriors were killed, and they have augmented their breeding stock with captives from other tribes, from Mexico, or from the white men.

"So if there is land to be taken, why not take it? The Indian would, and he often has. Man has done so from the beginning of time. None of us are where we once were, all have moved, all have merged."

"One day I shall go west, but when I go it will be to trade, not to conquer."

He shrugged. "As you will. My advice is to come with us. You could be of great service. Miss Majoribanks, as you may know, is searching for her brother. She may have to travel up many rivers before she finds him."

"If she does."

"You do not believe she will?" His eyes searched mine. "You are not hopeful?"

"There may be those who do not want him found, There may be some who would do anything to prevent his being found . . . at least, found alive."

"I think you are a fool," he said abruptly, "a fool with a wild imagination."

"The trouble with plotters," I said, "is that they always underrate their enemy, they assume others are less aware than they themselves, they believe they are moving in concealment when their every move is watched."

"Watched?"

"Seen, if you prefer the word. I do not believe those who plot have lived much in wild country. A city is the place to plot, not the mountains or the plains. There may be few about but everything that is actually seen is reported. There are simply too few men for their movements not to draw attention. It's not only the men but their tracks, why, there are Indian trackers who can tell every move, and can surmise from the moves what is planned. The Indian knows what is happening in his country, to survive he must know. So, he watches, often from a distance."

For the first time I thought him a little uneasy. He shrugged. "It is no business of mine. You will not join us then?"

"I cannot."

"Well, goodbye then." He held out his hand, and I almost took it. Yet there was something in the way he had set his feet that warned me, and I should have had to shift the gun to my left hand

"Goodbye," I said quietly, "and my best wishes to Miss Majoribanks." Then, I thought to jolt him a little, perhaps warn him enough so he would make no move against her, if that was in his mind. "By the way," I said casually, "did you know that Simon Tate rode east with a message from her?"

He had his hand on the latch and he froze in place. "Tate? Simon Tate? Who is he?"

"He was the inn-keeper back at the town where we met her. He is quite influential, politically. He rode off to the east to meet with some political or military friend. He seemed in great haste."

Macklem went out and closed the door behind him and I waited for an instant, then barred the door and went back to bed. Yet for a long time, I remained awake.

Macklem was a determined man. My bet was that he was allied with those planning some move in the west, with this mysterious Baron Torville, and he was a man not to be stopped by words. Now he had a steamboat to carry himself, his men and his rifles to where he was going, a steamboat to use for his own if he could take it from Tabitha Majoribanks. There was no other steamboat closer than New Orleans of which I knew. Well, there might be others, I supposed . . . but where?

It was long before I slept.

WHEN DAWN CAME, a thin gray light showed across the window and awakened me. For a moment I lay still, remembering my visitor, and thinking of Tabitha, for that was what I now called her, in my thoughts, at least.

Yet why? What was she to me? She did not like me. She, in fact, disliked me.

Oh, she had beautiful shoulders, a lovely face, and a proud set to the way she carried her head. She had something . . . something for somebody else, not me.

Perhaps for Rodney Macklem.

I sat up abruptly, so irritated by the thought that my

bare feet hit the cold floor before I realized. Hastily I pulled them up, and then began putting on my socks.

There was a quick rap on the door. I got up and unbarred it.

Jambe-de-Bois was there, looming huge in the door in his greasy cloak, his long hair straggling about his face, eyes wild.

"They've gone! You let them go!"

Swiftly I turned to the window. Where the steamboat had been there was nothing. The dock-side was empty, and upon the river there was nothing, no boat, no trail of smoke.

Something sank within me. They were gone. She was gone.

CHAPTER XIII

JAMBE-DE-BOIS LEANED OVER the table. I had never seen him so agitated. "You do not know him! He is a devil, this Macklem! A devil!"

"What could I do? I went to her and she would not listen. He was here last night, and—"

The expression on his face stopped me. "Macklem was *here*? To see you? Oh, my friend!"

When I told him what Macklem had wanted, he nodded his head. "Of course! He has her, her boat, and he has Macaire. Once he gets you, and perhaps the rest of us, he will be finished, the slate will be clean."

"What slate? What are you talking about?"

"Who can connect him with Foulsham . . . you, maybe me. Who is going west after Charles Majoribanks . . . his *sister*. If Charles does not escape, and the sister does not get back, if Macaire, in whom she might have confided, does not get back, then you and I are all that remain."

Irritably, I brushed it off. "You assume too much. We *know* nothing! We suspect much, but we know nothing at all. I cannot connect him with the murder of Foulsham, only that he was in the vicinity."

He turned abruptly and stared from the window. "He did not remember me," he muttered, "or if he remembered, he did not care! What could I do? Of what could I accuse him without in turn accusing myself?"

I sighed. There was something here I had to get to the bottom of. "Let's have something to eat," I said, "some coffee, at least."

We went down the stairs and sat at a table in the corner from which both the door to the street and to the kitchen were visible. Jambe placed his scarred fingers on the edge of the table, and I looked searchingly into his eyes. "You know Macklem, Jambe-de-Bois . . . what is it you know?"

"Too much!" he said. "I am a bad man, *mon ami,* but I am not an evil one!"

"There is a difference?" I asked.

He nodded, seriously. "Much difference! Much! Sometimes one is bad. One steals, one kills when fighting, one takes a ship here and there, but what one does is done in heat, it is done sword in hand against other swords, pistol against pistol, fist against fist.

"So, I have been a thief but, let me tell you something, *mon ami,* the poor rarely steal. Few steal to eat but men steal to buy wine, to buy women, to appear bold and free with money! Thievery is mostly from the cheapest of motives . . . to show off! To get by without work. So . . . I say this who have been a thief since childhood, and a pirate.

"But never have I killed just to be killing! Never have I held in contempt a human life! Never have I tortured; never have I abused the helpless! Macklem is evil! He is cold, vicious, without heart or scruple. He despises men, and despises women even more. He uses them, then kills them to show he is free of them, to show them his contempt!

"It is the proud, the beautiful, the aristocratic whom he would destroy . . . but not until he had seen them in the dirt, despised by all! I think he hates all men and women of breeding!

"The girl . . . the daughter of Majoribanks. Her he will take pleasure in destroying. And you. He will never rest until he destroys you because to this moment you are free of him. His promises failed, his effort to have you beaten in the street failed.

"So yes, I know him. But I do not think he now knows me. At first . . . well, I was afraid, for I know the man. I who have feared little, fear him.

"I was younger then, without this beard, without this gold ring in my ear, and with two strong legs.

"He has been what he is from a very young child. He was so in the slums, yet his beauty of body won him attention, he was given a chance, he was taken into a wealthy home and educated, yet when the time came he tortured and killed his benefactors. He escaped to sea . . . he betrayed his ship, took the money and went ashore and took a new name.

"Since then there have been many such actions. He has betrayed, defiled, ruined, and always with an easy smile, with laughter even, and many times he has been on the verge of great wealth, but always something has defeated him.

"We came ashore on an island in the eastern waters, came ashore with treasure. Eight of us came to bury it . . . and he brought a lunch, and several bottles of wine.

"We drank the wine. I drank little because I was young and it was food I wanted. I stole meat from the basket and when I thought I had been seen I threw it quickly down. Later I returned for a second chance but the basket was gone. I looked for the meat I had thrown down and there beside it was a rat . . . a dying rat, kicking its life out . . . poisoned.

"Turning, I ran back down the beach. All were drinking, most were drunk. I shouted at them, but they were eating also, and when I shouted again, Macklem turned deliberately and lifted a pistol to fire.

"I had two strong legs in those days, and I turned and dove into the brush and the bullet cut a leaf above my head.

"I ran and ran . . . he did not follow. And behind me I heard the screams of the dying. He had poisoned them all.

"For three days he hunted me. Twice, knowing I would be hungry, he left poisoned food upon the beach. The rats and gulls died, but not I . . . finally, he left."

"And the treasure?"

"He was no fool. He took it with him. He has the strength of four men, believe me. He carried the treasure back to the sloop we had taken. That sloop was nimble enough to get us aboard larger vessels where we did our thieving at gun point and slipped away. Our crew was sadly depleted, first by battle, then by scurvy, and some had been lost at sea . . . two lost overboard at night; no doubt his doing.

"After seven long months I was picked up, and since then have occasionally heard of him, and several times I have seen him. I have searched for him, followed him, learned some of his story . . . and waiting for the moment when I might see him die."

"Because he marooned you?"

"That, and my brother. The captain of that sloop, one of those poisoned, was my brother. I have waited, waited to see this man who now calls himself Macklem, die . . . but he does not die. With any weapon he is a master. I have never seen his equal. Believe me, do not provoke him. He will kill you."

"I am not so sure."

"Be sure. But you see? This is the man with whom we have left Miss Majoribanks . . . this is the man."

Since we had come downstairs an idea had been brewing, an idea based on the little I knew of the first voyage of the *Western Engineer*. "Think of this . . . by steamboat it is thirty-five days to St. Louis. Say he cuts the time to thirty. He still must go south and west to the Mississippi, and then come back north."

"So?"

"Over land, with horses, say it is six hundred miles. With average luck, twenty-five days, with the best of luck and fresh horses along the way . . . good horses . . . perhaps ten, fifteen days."

His fingers gripped my wrist. "You mean it? You will go?"

I nodded.

As we ate I considered all aspects of the journey before us. We must cross at least six hundred miles of rough country, and the distance was only a guess, gambling on finding horses we could exchange for those we rode. The horses I had chosen were tough, and already seasoned by their journey from Maine . . . it might be they could stand up to the march.

They were no stable-fed, carefully nurtured horses, but a tough, sturdy breed accustomed to hard usage and browsing where chance offered. Off-hand the longest day's travel on the way down had been forty miles, although distance was rarely reckoned in miles, only in time consumed.

Much would depend upon the weather, stream-crossings, and the fortunes of the way. If we were lucky, we could do it with time to spare.

I placed a couple of gold coins on the table. "Buy food. The simpler the better. We will want coffee, and what can be easily packed and prepared. I shall go see Mr. Dill."

Dill was in his office and I wasted no time nor did I keep anything to myself. He was a solid citizen, a respected, worthy man and I told him exactly what the problem was, even to what we suspected about Macklem, and what Jambe-de-Bois had told me, leaving out his own role.

"Go," Dill said, "and luck to you." He got to his feet. "This is my country, too, young man, and much of our future depends on the development of the Louisiana Territory.

"I've dozens of horses, and you'll need strong stock." He stepped to the door of his office and motioned to a clerk. "John, go to the stables and have Joel put lead ropes on Sam and Dave. Mr. Talon here will take them."

By mid-afternoon we were across the river and headed west.

Yet what Dill had said remained in my mind. He had said this was his country, too. Was it mine? By birth I was a Canadian, but now I was here, and was this not my country also?

For me travelling was no new thing. On the Gaspe Peninsula of Quebec where I was born there was not much work. My family owned land there, but to work as a shipwright demanded long trips. Several times I had been down the coast to the towns of Maine, I had worked in Nova Scotia. My first trip to Toronto had been with my father and uncle while I was a very young boy. We had worked all summer at Lachine, near Montreal, building several bateaux. These were forty feet long, eight feet wide, with almost vertical sides and a blunt bow and stern. We built the sides of fir, the bottom of oak. These boats were occasionally sailed, more often rowed or poled, and when close in shore, pulled by men walking in shallow water near the shore. Later we helped build one of the first Durham boats to be used in Canada. These were eighty to ninety feet overall with a beam of ten feet, and were usually sailed or rowed. They could carry thirty-five to forty tons of freight down-stream, eight to ten tons up-stream. Both types of boat were much used on lakes and rivers in Canada.

My father had helped to build the *Toronto Yacht*, working on it in 1798 and 1799 for several months. In its time it was the sleekest, fastest craft on the lakes, and when she was wrecked in 1812 he had been very unhappy for days.

He was a man proud of his work, taking great care in the shaping of every timber, and every craft built by his hands always remained in his heart. He had come home to Perce, disappointed and angry. He had been asked to work on a twenty-two-gun ship, but after seeing the design, refused.

"They are fools!" he told my mother. "Fools! She will never stand a rough sea. They do not know the lakes, these men. They think we have a lot of mill-ponds here.

And the timber! Much of it is not seasoned, but they will go ahead."

"And we needed the money," my mother said.

"Aye!" he muttered gloomily. "But I will have no part in a thing badly built. Men will die because of it, but regardless of that, a man does not waste the trees it took God centuries to grow in building something of no account.

"Remember that, my boy," he rested his hand on my shoulder, "the wood with which we work has strength, it has beauty, it has resilience! If it is treated well, it will last many, many years! If you build, build well. No job must be slackly done, no good material used badly. There is beauty in building, but build to last, so that generations yet to come will see the pride with which you worked.

"There are proud ones who look with disdain upon a man who works with his hands. Do not do so. It is not every man who can shape a timber or build a bridge or ship. Work with honor, my son, and build with beauty and strength."

We brought our bateau down from Lachine on that first trip and tied up at Allan's Wharf, which some people were beginning to call Merchant's Wharf, at the foot of Frederick Street.

It was always a good day when my father reached Toronto for at some time during his stay he would enjoy a drink with Dr. Baldwin, an Irishman who knew much about building, and he often came to watch when my father was building a squared-log house. Such houses demanded the master craftsman, for each log must be precisely squared and shaped. My father was such a man.

Jambe-de-Bois swore very little. Our trip from Canada had accustomed him to riding but he still did not like it, yet he was going west to reach St. Louis before the steamboat, and he did like that.

We rode until sundown, then changed to our new mounts and rode on until midnight. We camped in a forest of towering trees, gathering broken branches for fuel, and at daybreak we were off again. At noon we switched horses again. As evening came on we stopped in a meadow, watered and curried our horses, then turned them loose in the meadow to graze.

The roads and trails were dry; the weather cool. We had no trouble. Several times we stopped at farm-houses, and once at an inn. For seven days we rode hard, stopping now and again to sleep and rest the horses, eating when we could find the time. We came on the morning of the eighth day into a little hollow where a small stream ran southwestward through a meadow. It was an area where the forest was thinning out, the big trees growing fewer and fewer.

Some sense was warning me, a feeling like that back in the forests of Maine that I had seen or heard something my mind had not completely dealt with. Turning I went down off the ridge along which we were riding and through the trees into the meadow.

Jambe-de-Bois pulled up beside me, easing himself in the saddle. "Stoppin'?"

"Just an idea. Regardless, the horses are ga'nted and we could all do with rest."

We rode through the water of the creek into a small

grove along its edge. Hidden by brush and the over-hang of the trees, we swung down, stripped the gear from our horses and picketed them behind the trees in a corner of the meadow.

Jambe stretched out on a grassy slope in the shade of an elm, and I walked off a bit, picking a few berries left on the bushes. In doing so I drew near the trail we had followed to this place, although I was concealed from it by thick brush. In the distance I heard the hoofs of an approaching horse. And then . . . several horses.

"Wait," someone said, and the first horse went on ahead, but returned. "There is nothing. I can see for several miles. They are further ahead than we thought."

"We'll come up with them tonight . . . and it must be tonight, Jem. You know what the Colonel said. And I'd cross the devil himself sooner 'n him."

Now I could see them through the brush. There were four men. One rode a fine dapple-gray gelding. He was a thin, rail-like man who could have weighed nothing but he had two knives in his belt and long, tapering fingers that kept dropping to the knives with a caressing touch.

I could not see his face, nor the face of one other. But there was a burly, red-haired man with greasy buckskins and a man in a black slouch hat and homespun pants who had a wide grin but few teeth. There was a bend in his nose and a scar over his eyes. He looked like a man who would hunt trouble.

Holding very still, I waited. Then I inched my hand to my belt-gun and drew it, waiting. If they saw anything suspicious, I would kill one of them without hesitating. The shot would also be a warning to Jambe-de-Bois.

But after letting their horses catch their wind, they

moved on. Fortunately, the man in the greasy buckskins was a talker, and none of them noticed where we had turned off. So, on down the trail they went.

"Jambe?" I spoke softly as I approached. "Get the horses. We're moving out."

He groaned, sitting up. Briefly, I explained and he went at once for the reluctant horses.

"What now?"

"That way." I pointed into the woods.

"But there's no trail!"

"That's right. There is no trail. We'll make our own."

I checked the pistol I carried, then my rifle.

"Jambe?" I described them. "If we see them, don't wait, don't talk . . . shoot them on sight."

CHAPTER XIV

St. Louis was bathed in moonlight when we finally arrived, crossing the river on a flat-boat we happened to see making ready on the east bank. We were landed on a shelving shore away from the streets, which was what we wanted, hoping to arrive without being seen.

On a side street we found a man leading a team into a barn. A lantern hung over the door, another inside.

"Is this a livery stable?" I asked.

He was a well set-up man of perhaps fifty. "No," he glanced at us, then at our horses. "However, I've got some empty stalls and a corral. Cost you two-bits a night down at one of them stables in town. I'll board the lot of them for a dollar a week."

"You've got yourself a deal."

We dismounted and stripped our gear from the horse and carried it inside. I handed the man a dollar.

"We want to put up at a quiet place," I said. "Got any ideas?"

"Sure have. Mary O'Brien, Ma, we call her. She lives right down the street. Fourth house from here. Her husband was lost on the river and her boys have gone down to N' Orleans. She's a fine woman, and she can use the money."

The house was sparsely furnished with home-made

furniture except for a big old chest of drawers. It was neat . . . everything was spotless.

When I commented her blue eyes twinkled. "Mister," she said, "I got nothing else to do but clean. I sew a mite, but there's little enough of that to do and my sewin's not fancy.

"Board an' room, two dollars a week for each. I know that seems expensive but folks are crowdin' St. Louis right now, an' grub's expensive. Why, sugar's gone to thirty-five cents a pound an' coffee's fifty cents the pound."

"That's mighty expensive, ma'am," I agreed.

"Expensive! I should say! Why, Eddie, that's my boy, he's got a fine education. Seven years of schoolin'! *Seven,* mind you! But what can he earn? Ten dollars a month in the winter teachin' school, an' eight dollars a month in summer helpin' the tavern-keeper! Him an' Joe, that's my other boy, they taken a load of logs down river. Figure to sell them at a profit. If'n they just git back, all right. N' Orleans they tell me is a sinful city!"

"Terrible!" I said, speaking from no experience. "As much as a man's soul is worth just to go there."

Jambe-de-Bois gave me a disgusted look, and I handed her four dollars. "That's the first week, we're good eaters."

"Like to see a man eat hearty. Does my heart good."

"Now tell me, Mrs. O'Brien," I asked. "If I wanted to go someplace where I could hear the news, where would it be?"

"Choteau's." She paused a moment, looking from one to the other. "On the other hand, I'd say if y' was listenin' for the kind o' talk that leads to no good, I'd say Pierre's, on the Rue de la Tour. It is only a few steps beyond the corner.

"But have a hand to your money, if y' have any. My old man used to hang about there but he'd nothing to lose, and he always claimed Pierre, at least, was an honest man."

"We'll go along then. And could we bring you a bit of something, Mrs. O'Brien?"

"Git along with you! I'll just set up with my bit o' coffee."

PIERRE'S WAS A place of wooden tables and benches, and Pierre was a stocky man with a healthy stomach hanging over pants cut off below the knees and a wide belt that struggled to retain the stomach.

The place was empty, and for a few minutes we talked in French, then Pierre reverted to English. "It will be the only tongue soon. It's an American land we have now. Once there were French wherever a man looked, up the river and down, now there's only a few of us left."

He glanced from Jambe-de-Bois to me. "Jean Daniel Talon. It is a good name. There was a Talon once who was a pirate, I think."

"Aye," I said dryly, "he was the first of our line, and might be better able to face what we have before us than we. There's a steamer coming up the river . . . it used to be called the *Western Engineer*."

"The sea serpent?" He chuckled. "I fancied that one! I'd like to have owned her myself. She runs a high-pressure engine and a paddle-wheel astern, specially designed for the western rivers."

"We came overland to get here first." Then I outlined the story for him, and when I finished, he looked carefully about.

"I am an honest man, so they tell me nothing but I can hear, and I hear a great deal. Men have come to St. Louis and they have disappeared inland . . . a few at a time . . . fifty or a hundred in all.

"There are rumors something is in the wind, but there are always such rumors. I believe none of them."

"You're empty tonight?"

He scowled. "Yes, and I don't understand it. Most of the time there's twenty-five to thirty men in here. Of course, it's late."

I got up. "Pierre, we're dead beat and we're going to turn in. We'll be at Mary O'Brien's if there's news, but tell nobody where we are unless a man named Macaire should show up."

We went off, and at the corner, paused a moment. It was cool. A gentle wind was coming up the river carrying a faint suggestion of wood-smoke.

Jambe-de-Bois looked around, impatiently. "It's no good place," he said. "We'd best be gettin' on."

Yet I hesitated a moment longer. Had that been a shadow in a doorway. I reached inside my coat for the pistol, rested my hand upon it. Slowly then, I turned to follow him.

They came out of the darkness with a rush. Only a whisper of moccasins on the boardwalk or in the dust. They were already hidden in the shadows waiting for us, and they closed in fast.

My pistol came out and I fired. There was no chance to miss, the man was almost within arm's length of me when the gun went off. He stopped in full stride, his coat aflame from the blast of black powder, and then he fell.

A sweeping blow with the barrel of the pistol dropped another one and then I jammed the muzzle of the pistol into the throat of a third.

Jambe-de-Bois had turned like lightning, I never dreamed he could move with such speed. He was cutting and stabbing with a long knife. There was a picket fence where we had been attacked and we put our backs to it.

Somebody struck the knife from Jambe-de-Bois' hand and it went flying. They closed in, I punched and kicked. I saw Jambe fall back against the fence. He struck out with his fist, then stooped and when I momentarily fought myself clear I saw he was laying about him with his wooden leg!

Catching a man by the throat with my left hand I lifted him clear of the ground and shoved him into the face of another, then rushed them both off their feet. I took a savage blow to the kidney. Turning, I struck the man along the temple, with the edge of my hand. Another charged in low and I brought a knee up into his face slamming down on the back of his head as my knee came up. He grunted and fell, his nose crushed.

I took a wicked blow, a dozen men struck at me it seemed, and then I was hitting, driving at them, punching low and hard. I butted one man, kicked another, and suddenly I stood alone, gasping for breath. At least three men lay on the ground, one of them the man I'd shot.

Jambe-de-Bois held to the picket-fence with one hand and his peg-leg in the other.

"There must have been a dozen," I said.

"Seemed like it, but I figure only nine," he commented,

"and they weren't much. In the old days at sea, they'd have lasted no time at all. Why, the crew of the—"

He shut up suddenly. "You're a fighter," he said, and he was smiling, the first time I remembered seeing him smile. "It was a pleasure to be with you."

The dark street was empty. Pistol shots at night were no new thing in St. Louis where drunken trappers on the way home often fired their guns out of sheer good spirits.

With my toe I rolled over the man I'd shot. He was dead, all right, and he was one of those I'd seen following us on the way west. Near him lay my gun. I picked it up and thrust it into my waist-band.

One of the men, badly hurt, started to rise. Jambe-de-Bois hefted his peg-leg. "Lie still, damn you," he said conversationally, "or I'll smash your skull."

The man ceased to move. Jambe-de-Bois rolled him over on his back. "If you live," he said quietly, "don't let me see you again or I'll split you like an over-ripe melon."

He strapped on his leg. I watched him, wondering how many times that piece of oak had come off in brawls. It made a terrible weapon at close quarters, and wherever else he was, Jambe-de-Bois was a mighty fighter. With him around, as long as he was on my side, I need never worry about my back.

We limped home. Somehow I'd been kicked on the leg, although I did not remember it, and when I looked into the mirror in my room I found a welt on my cheekbone and a lump over one eye.

Jambe-de-Bois dropped on his bed and stared at me. "Y' look to have been fightin', man," he said, and chuckled. "Best fight I've had in a year! But you did us a service when y' shot the first one."

"You think so?"

"Aye. 'Tis my thought that he was the leader an' the paymaster as well. When y' downed him it taken the heart from some o' them for they were not sure when they'd be paid . . . if ever."

"I couldn't miss," I said. "He came right at me."

"Aye, y' couldn't miss y' say, but the fact is, y' didn't. The man's dead an' we're alive an' that's the crux o' the matter."

For two days we loitered about, each going his own way, each listening. We heard nothing. It was true that men had appeared, bought lead for bullets, powder, and some food and then had dropped from sight, but nobody knew anything substantial, or if they did know, they preferred not to speak.

At night we avoided troublesome places, and retired early.

Late one night after we had retired, there was a light knock on the door. It was Mary O'Brien.

"It is Pierre," she whispered. "Come!"

He was in the kitchen, with a cup of Mary's coffee.

"The steamboat," he said, low-voiced, "has come. It is about four or five miles up the river at a small island off the mouth of Coldwater Creek. A boat has come down from the steamboat to the town, and has landed at the mouth of La Petite Riviere . . . the one they are now calling Mill Creek."

"Who has landed?"

"Two gentlemen, and a lady. They are on the street now."

Tabitha was here. She was in St. Louis . . . would she listen to me now?

CHAPTER XV

CHOTEAU WAS NOW the man I most wanted to see. Laclede had founded the town, but it was Choteau who had been its heart and mind since, and it was around his fur trading establishment that the town revolved. At my suggestion Jambe-de-Bois kept himself hidden at Mary O'Brien's. Out on the street I paused, getting my bearings. Carefully, I studied the faces. I must not come upon any of them without warning.

My presence could mean nothing but a declaration of war. He would know that I had arranged to build a boat in Pittsburgh, thus if I had come west it could only be because of an interest in his activities or those of Tabitha Majoribanks, which in effect were the same thing.

Despite the hour the streets were busy; there were wagons drawn by mules or oxen, men riding horses, Indians of several tribes, trappers in buckskins, traders from the east or up from New Orleans, a mixed lot, but all rough, and capable. There was excitement in the air. The very thought that beyond lay the wilderness, the unknown lands of mountain and plain, generated such excitement.

I stepped back against the face of a building and looked left and right, scanning the crowd and the buildings opposite. I had the uncomfortable sense of being watched. But I saw no familiar face, and again turned toward

Choteau's. In my belt I carried Foulsham's pistol, in a sheath I carried a knife that had been in the family for at least two hundred years, a knife of such steel as I had never found elsewhere, a knife made in India, taken from the castle of Gingee by my ancestor.

I paused again, pretending to check out various stores and shops along the way. I entered several, looked around, watching the street as I did so. Two men had come up in the street opposite the store and stopped there, leaning on the hitching rail and talking. From time to time they stole quick looks at the place I had entered.

Standing at the counter I bought tobacco, which I did not use but which Jambe-de-Bois would enjoy, and paying for my purchase I walked through the gap between the counters and to the back of the store. There was an entrance there through which wagons were loaded and unloaded. I went out, closed the door behind me and walked swiftly down the alley, stepping around stacks of old lumber refuse, and piles of wood for winter burning.

Choteau was in his office when I entered, and he turned to study me. As to where he placed his loyalties, I did not know, but I had no choice but to explain fully. Quickly, I told him that Charles Majoribanks had stumbled upon knowledge of a plot to seize the Territory, that Tabitha Majoribanks was now in St. Louis en route to the west to find him, and that I suspected Colonel Macklem to be one of the plotters. I finished by saying that I was considering following them west and investigating the situation first hand.

"I am a fur trader, not a politician," he replied. "I know nothing of the situation you suggest. There have been, of course, several abortive attempts to seize Louisiana in one way or another, but they haven't a ghost of a chance."

"I have heard that the roughest and more desperate sort of men have been gathering in towns along the frontier, all awaiting some sort of news. The steamboat has at least twenty cases of rifles in its cargo," I explained. "The rifles are, no doubt, intended to arm renegade Indians, and I expect that vastly more powder and lead is aboard for the white men who have their own weapons. The more I think on it, the more I worry that this group intends to help finance its efforts by seizing furs coming down river."

He shrugged. "It is not easy to take furs from the kind of men who go up these rivers after them."

"But they have lost furs to Indians in the past?"

"Of course." Choteau tipped back in his chair, rubbing his chin thoughtfully. Then he shook his head. "I do not know you, Mr. Talon. I do not know you at all. You are a very young man who has come to me with a somewhat fanciful tale, that is all."

"You have met Charles Majoribanks?"

"He was entertained in my home when he accompanied the Yellowstone expedition aboard the *Western Engineer*."

"You did not entertain him on his return? Did you see him then?" I asked.

"No, as a matter of fact, I did not. It was my understanding that he had remained up country for the purpose of studying the plants, the animal life, or something."

"So you have not heard from him since his first visit?"

He shrugged again. "Should I have? As I am a very busy man, I cannot see all whom pass through St. Louis."

He studied me thoughtfully. "You must realize, Colonel Macklem has been in St. Louis several times. He is well thought of here. He has many friends. He is known along the Missouri River as well as the Platte. We have had no reason to complain of his conduct. From my perspective, it would also be difficult to 'seize' anything west of here. A bit like trying to seize steam. Without a very large and disciplined cadre of men, I cannot imagine it. This is not to say that no one would try, as I mentioned it has been attempted in the past. I simply find it unlikely."

For a moment I had nothing to say and suddenly all notions of plots began to seem rather childish. Yet one thing remained.

"You do not think it strange that the steamboat did not dock at St. Louis? That it proceeded up-stream to what is in effect a hiding place?"

He frowned momentarily. "Yes," he admitted, "that does seem a bit strange. No doubt they have their reasons."

"And there is the fact that Captain Foulsham was murdered while carrying information about such a plot. I suspect Foulsham had tracked Baron Torville from England or perhaps Europe."

"I know of that only from you. I have no reason to doubt your word, but on the other hand, many men are murdered while travelling. The Natchez Trace and the Wilderness Road are infamous for such things . . . so are our rivers."

He got to his feet. "It has been pleasant, Mr. Talon, but I have other duties. You will excuse me?"

—

I LEFT THE office and stood in the trade store watching the people, yet thinking of everything else. Was I a fool then? How much, really, did I know?

I thought of my own situation. What was I doing here? What had prompted me to leave a good job, one in which I might soon have become owner or part owner of a steamboat or a boat-yard, and come off to this far place? What did I know of Macklem, anyway?

Could it be that I was jealous? Did I fear him? He had destroyed Sam Purdy, a man reputed to be dangerous. He had easily won the confidence of Tabitha, who could barely stand my presence. He treated me when we were together with a kind of amused contempt . . . was that it?

If it was Tabitha, was I not trying to save a girl who did not wish to be saved? Or who arrogantly believed herself competent to handle her own affairs? And with her father's communications to read, did she not know much more than I about all that was taking place? Surely, in all that secret network of correspondents, some one of them would know something of Macklem?

A girl was serving coffee, tea and baked goods from behind a bar at the front of the store. It was a canny choice, for it brought people inside where they could view the merchandise. The crowd jostled past and around me but I paid little attention.

What was I doing here? Why had I ridden across such a great distance to get here? I felt like a fool, a colossal fool. I should have stayed in Pittsburgh, building boats.

"Quite an odd lot, aren't they?"

Startled, I turned to see a young man beside me, a

slender, rather attractive young man with a nicely-boned aristocratic-looking face. He indicated the passersby. "I wanted to see this. I had to see it. Now that I'm here, I find it hard to believe . . . the redskins, and all."

"This is their country," I commented. "You should expect to find them here."

"Oh, but I did! It's just the reality of it all. Why, we used to play Red Indians when I was a child in England, but to think I am here and some of them are warriors who have probably taken human scalps—"

"And would again tomorrow if the chance offered," I said. "It still happens, you know, just a few miles west."

"Yes, I suppose it does." He turned and extended a hand. "I am Donald McQuarrie. I am trying to get on with one of the fur companies, with Choteau, if he'll have me."

"My name is Talon," I said.

He nodded. "So I was told."

"Told?" I stared at him.

"Mr. Choteau told me who you were, what you looked like. He said I should talk to you."

"I am not a fur trader. I've no jobs to offer," I said, "and my meeting with Mr. Choteau was very brief. I do not believe he was much impressed."

"On the contrary." McQuarrie watched the crowd, his eyes alert and busy. "The Choteaus have been around for a long, long time. There's talent in the blood, and a good deal of native shrewdness.

"You see," he paused, watching the crowd, "I'd been to see him just before you, and about much the same thing."

For a moment what he said did not register. "Much the same thing?"

"I followed you west, and I might say, had a devil of a time at it. When you travel you do not waste time. You just about succeeded in losing me a couple of times."

"You followed us?"

"You . . . yes, I did. You see, when Simon Tate reached Boston, I was there. The gentleman to whom he went on arrival was a friend of mine, and I had let him know why I was in America. He let me see the papers Tate had, and Tate told me of you, and here I am."

"Might I ask why?"

"Obvious, is it not? I want Macklem, I want him very badly indeed. Most of all, I want Torville."

"There is a connection then?"

He glanced at me. "Of course. You see, we don't like Torville. He's a dangerous, completely unscrupulous man. He has betrayed the French, and he betrayed us. He has no loyalty but to himself. Now he is here."

McQuarrie talked well and he made sense of a kind, yet I did not trust him. He was apparently British, and he had that manner that one recognizes as a product of the better schools. We see quite a few of their type in Canada. Many of our most and least successful pioneers had been retired British officers.

"Where do you stand?" I asked bluntly. "This is all very well but I know you no more than Choteau knew me."

"I am a brother officer of Captain Robert F. Foulsham. In fact, he was a year or two ahead of me in school. We were on the same mission, actually."

He glanced at me. "Ever hear of Lord Selkirk?"

"Of course."

"He established a colony west of the Great Lakes, if you'll recall."

"I know the story. It was attacked, some said by the *metis,* or Indians . . . I have forgotten the details. But wasn't it nearly destroyed?"

"It was. And although he never appeared on the scene, Torville was responsible. He was one of those who stirred up the trouble. The Hudson Bay Company wanted no settlers coming into the area who might interfere with their fur trade. As it was, they had complete control. Then Selkirk entered the picture. Yet there might have been no trouble had it not been for Torville, who wanted no settlers there either and for his own reasons."

"What reasons?"

"Think . . . the fur cannot last forever, and when the fur trade is no longer profitable, the Hudson Bay Company will relinquish its authority. Into that vacuum, a man of will, authority and determination might step."

"He's mad."

"Perhaps . . . but uncommonly shrewd as well, and he knows how to use the passions, discontents and greed of other men. Our belief is that he has support from quite a number of wealthy, power-hungry men in both Europe and America. Until such a time as your army has posts and forts in the Louisiana Territory there will always be those who will plot to seize it."

So here I was, back in the middle of it again, just when I was thinking of returning to Pittsburgh. And that would, no doubt, still be the best thing for me.

A disturbing thought came to me. Had Tabitha's father, with his chain of correspondents, been one of those backing Torville? Was her taking Macklem on as captain of her boat no accident, but a matter of design? In this wide open land full of possibilities it had come to that . . . I had no idea of what to believe.

"What a small world, after all!" The voice was cynical, amused. "Tabitha, will you look now? It is the young man from the trail! The one who was going to remain in Pittsburgh? I wonder what brings him to St. Louis?"

I turned. It was Macklem. And beside him, Tabitha.

CHAPTER XVI

On this day Macklem wore a handsomely tailored suit. He was taller than I and I found it irritated me, for he moved in close and seemed to be trying to use his height to intimidate.

It was not only his height, but everything about him seemed calculated to impress, or such was the feeling I got. Previously when we met we had both been dressed for travel so perhaps it was the clothes, perhaps some other quality, or some deeply rooted instinct that caused my hackles to rise.

Tabitha extended her hand. "It *is* good to see you!" she said, and surprisingly, I believe she meant it. "Are you shopping?"

"Sight-seeing," I said. When I thought of McQuarrie and turned to introduce him, he was gone.

"What is it?" Macklem said. "You look surprised."

"Surprised to see you. Somehow I thought you'd be far up the river by now."

"We're only going to be here today and tomorrow," Tabitha said. "We're in need of some supplies, and I want to see if there's any news of Charles." And then she added, "Colonel Macklem has been helping me."

"Well, he looks like he was born for the job," I said, and felt better when his features tightened.

"Just what does that mean?" he asked abruptly. For the first time I seemed to have gotten under his hide.

He was a proud man, and a touchy one, not at all as sure of himself as he seemed. For some reason what I had said touched a nerve, and it was a thing to remember.

"Where is Miss Higgs?" I said.

"She's aboard the boat," Tabitha said. "She wasn't feeling well."

"Perhaps I could go see her," I said cheerfully. "I am sorry."

"Oh, but you can't," Tabitha said, "the boat is—"

Macklem interrupted. "She's not receiving visitors."

"Alright then, another time."

Just at that moment a man came up and touched me on the sleeve. "Mr. Talon? Mr. Choteau would like to see you. When it is possible."

Tabitha stared at me, coldly curious. "Talon? But I thought your name was Daniel?"

"Jean Daniel Talon," I said.

Macklem's attention had sharpened. "Talon? I know that name."

"It is possible," I said, then added, "Well, please give Miss Higgs my regards?"

"I shall," Tabitha said, then suddenly she turned to Macklem. "Colonel, I must see Mr. Choteau myself. Shall I meet you at the dock then? In two hours?"

He was caught completely off-guard. I think he had no intention of letting her out of his sight, that he had planned to carefully manage the trip ashore so that she talked to no one when he was not present. But here in the crowded trade store, with a member of Choteau's management standing nearby, his ability to control her was limited unless he wished to make a scene that might set the community against him.

"Can't we do that later?" There was irritation in his tone, "I mean, there's much to do, and—"

"Do what you must, Colonel. Mr. Talon will escort me as he is going to see Mr. Choteau himself. This is the perfect place to get what I need for myself and for Mrs. Higgs. So then . . . in two hours?"

Abruptly she turned her back on him and took my arm. When I glanced back he was still standing near the door, staring after us, and I chuckled.

"You must have ridden very fast," she said.

"Yes, we did. I wanted to get here before you did."

"Why?"

The question stopped me. Finally I said, "Because I thought you might need help and I wanted to be near if you needed me."

"That was sweet. You know, Mr. Talon, you can be very nice at times . . . and very unpleasant at others."

"Then we are two of a kind," I said.

She stifled a laugh and looked away so that I couldn't see her face.

"Have you news of your brother?"

"No," she said. "That is one reason I wish to see Mr. Choteau."

We were shown into his presence at once. When he saw Tabitha he bowed deeply. "This can only be Miss Majoribanks?"

"How do you do?" She accepted the chair he held for her, then looked up at him. "Is there any word of my brother Charles? Anything at all?"

"Nothing, I've sent scouts up the Missouri and up the

Platte. They will make inquiries. The last we heard of him he was on the Kansas River near the Missouri, gathering plants."

"I must find him."

He fussed with the papers on his desk. "You must not think of it. Stay with us in St. Louis, Miss Majoribanks. We will find him. It is vast country out there, so vast you cannot even imagine it. Looking for a needle in a haystack would be simplicity itself by comparison."

"Nevertheless, I shall go. Charles, if he is not injured, will find *me*. He will hear of our steamboat, surely there cannot be two such in the world, and he will come to it. If for no other reason than he travelled on it before and he must dispose of the samples he has taken."

"If he is free," I said.

She turned sharply, "What do you know about that?"

"No more than you have said. Charles may have been captured," I replied. "Only that."

"And what is your interest in this?" she asked sharply. "As I understand it, you are not even an American. You are a Canadian."

"This trouble may cross many borders, I think," I said quietly. "Already the British are involved and possibly the French. As for myself, I am a man who believes in order. Only through a just order are we permitted the freedom of action and thought that allow us any kind of peace in which to work. Canadian or not, I would rather see this problem handled by the United States than the agents of a European empire, though we may need their help. I fear foreign influences might ultimately make the problem worse and I have heard that some of those influences may be at work on both sides of this question."

"You mean backing this Baron Torville?"

"Yes. And there are agents of the crown pursuing him. I have personally met two of them. Torville is an adventurer, pure and simple. One of those, no doubt, who still lives in the thinking of William the Conqueror or those Normans who invaded Sicily and set up a kingdom there. Perhaps he sees himself as a revolutionary but I doubt it. He is more the type who comes afterward. Idealistic revolution always gives way to the brutes, the strongmen. In France, for example. Those who created the revolution, its initial leaders, all ended up as victims of it, and who reaped the benefit . . . the General, Napoleon. Torville, however he sees himself, is as out of date as a fossil, sir, but does not realize it."

Choteau looked at me thoughtfully, and I think Tabitha was surprised as well. "You seem well-informed, young man."

"I am not. I am only accidentally involved in something I do not completely understand. But you called me here to speak to me, and I have no interest in wasting your time. What is it?"

"You suggested you might be going west. It occurred to me that you might be better armed . . . I do not know what weapons you have, but am sure you have nothing as fine as what I have here.

"It happens that a young Austrian of great wealth came to hunt buffalo. He wished also to kill a grizzly bear. He brought excellent weapons, much equipment . . . and then he became ill.

"This was months ago, and now he has sent word to sell his weapons and equipment. Since you are going alone into such a dangerous area, I suspect you might be interested."

"I am definitely interested."

He stepped to the door. "Jacques? Show Mr. Talon the Pauly rifle and Collier pistols, will you, please?"

I followed Jacques. When the door closed behind me, I wondered if Choteau was not equally eager to get me out of the room so he might talk to Tabitha without being overheard. In any event, I had no excuse to remain, and the guns did interest me.

Jacques was envious. "I should like to own them," he said, "but I have not the money. It is much, very, very much."

"Tell me who made them."

"Pauly was a Swiss, from Bern or near there, and he served in the Swiss army, then moved to France. The cartridges are internally primed using a substance called . . ." Jacques referred to a piece of paper ". . . potassium chlorate. At a demonstration before one of Napoleon's generals Pauly fired twenty-two shots in two minutes."

The rifle felt good in my hands, a slender, graceful weapon. The barrel drops forward and you put in your cartridge. It uses less powder and will not hang fire, and it can be loaded or unloaded with great speed.

"And here are two Collier patent pistols, with five shot cylinders."

They were going to cost me more than I could afford, but how much is a man's life worth? I hesitated, but held the rifle in my hands while I considered, and was reluctant to put it down. It had a nice feel, moving easily to the shoulder, the sight was good. At last I set it on the table.

Taking up the pistols, I studied them: The Collier had

a hand-turned cylinder that locked into position and an ingenious priming system. They would be complex and slow to reload once their cylinders and priming reservoirs had been emptied but until that moment their rate of fire would be unprecedented. Jacques carefully demonstrated their mechanism as well as how the rifle cartridges worked.

"How much?" I said at last, knowing they were too much. "You will have to talk to Mr. Choteau about that. They are at his disposal, and from what I hear, he can put upon them what price he wishes."

Reluctantly, I left the guns and walked back to the office. Tabitha was gone.

"Where is Miss Majoribanks?" I demanded.

"Wait!" Choteau said. "Just a minute, young man!"

"I must find her! She must not go back to that boat!"

"You will see her tonight. She has only gone to my home. We are to have a small, informal reception for her this evening, and we would be pleased if you would attend as well."

"Will Colonel Macklem be present tonight?"

"Of course. Do you object?"

"Certainly not. He will be your guest. I know little about the man, and certainly he conducts himself as a gentleman. Whatever differences we may have, they will not be settled in your home."

"Thank you." He paused. "Now as to your plans?"

Plans? I had no plans except to keep Tabitha out of trouble and to discover whatever Torville had in mind. And then to get back to building boats.

Choteau chuckled. "I'd say you had your work cut out for you. Have you ever been in a fight of this kind,

Mr. Talon? Torville will have some of the Indians with him, you know."

"I grew up among the Micmacs and the Hurons. Had dealings with a few Mohawks."

"Do you know any of the languages?"

"Sign language . . . some Delaware."

"Delaware? That's interesting. We have a number of them around here, you know. Some of our best trackers are Delawares."

Choteau got up. "It is growing late. Mr. Talon, my people have gone home, but come in tomorrow when Jacques can unpack the ammunition for you."

"I don't believe I can afford those guns, Mr. Choteau. Though they are perhaps the finest I've seen."

"Yes," Choteau leaned back in his chair, "they are excellent weapons. As a matter of fact, the price was left to my judgment for, to the owner, money has no meaning. He was more concerned the weapons be properly used. As long as your mission is the protection of Miss Majoribanks and the establishment of stability in our territory, the guns are yours."

CHAPTER XVII

AT MARY O'BRIEN'S, I changed into my dark suit. Jambe-de-Bois stared at my preparations with obvious disapproval. "It's no good thing y' do. Now he knows you'll be to the dinner tonight. Stay clear of the man, you don't let such as him know what you're about, lad. You don't. It's like baitin' a trap for yourself."

"I've got to warn her. Somehow I've got to get her to get rid of him."

"Huh! Y' tried that, and it came to nothing. The man is a charmer. He'll have her won over now, and you'll be shut out colder than ever. I say—don't go."

There was sense in what he was saying. Even as I arranged my cravat, I knew he was right, up to a point. But I was to see Tabitha, so little else mattered.

"Midnight," I told Jambe-de-Bois, "no later. I shall be back, and in the morning, I will go for the guns. With any luck she can be persuaded to stay here in St. Louis. Then we can try to find Torville's camp and free Miss Majoribank's brother. If nothing else we can report what we find to Choteau and, through him, the proper authorities."

"I like none of it."

"Rest easy . . . and if you see an Englishman about, one named McQuarrie, tell him to stand by."

"Aye," Jambe-de-Bois said gloomily. "If I see him, and if I see you. Protect yourself . . . I'll not say protect yourself in the clinches for there are no clinches with Macklem. He'll take you at long range if he can."

"You worry too much." I put my hand on his shoulder. "Rest easy, I say. I shall be back by midnight."

The street was dark when I stepped from the door, pausing a moment under the porch to look right and left. There was a faint smell of rain in the air, and a smell of other things as well, of wood-smoke, of fresh lumber, of the river. I walked into the street, glancing around again.

The shadow of the bluff left the street darker than the night around, yet I was close enough to the river to hear the creak of lines that tied the various craft to the shore. For a moment I stood still, drawing in the stillness, the coolness, the freshness of the air. The wind was blowing down river, coming from those strange, unknown lands that lay up-stream, where the Indian camp-fires were, and the buffalo wandered the plains in their uncounted millions.

Stepping through the gate, I closed it behind me and started up the walk. I had taken no more than three steps when I heard a faint, despairing cry.

I stopped, listening. Again I heard it, from the direction of the river. I waited.

No sound.

I started on, disturbed by that cry. Should I go down to the river? I was dressed for company, and the area was muddy, the wharf stacked with casks and bales. Then I heard the cry again, and turning quickly I hurried through the narrow lane to the water.

All was still. Pausing to listen I could only hear the lap of water about the hulls of the keel-boats . . . no other sound.

I was about to turn away when I heard, "*Please! Help me!*"

The call seemed to come from the water off the stern of the nearest keel-boat. Leaping to the bow I ran along the walk toward the stern. The cry came again, seemingly from the other side of the boat. I turned, bending to look over into the dark water.

At that instant there was a rush of feet behind me, I started to straighten, but a glancing blow from a club hit me on the head, my hat went flying, and dazed, I tried to get my hands up.

There were at least six and they all had clubs. Only their numbers saved me as they crowded for blows. I staggered, fell against the bulwark with blows battering at my head and arms. Dazed, and badly hurt, I tried to fight. The pressure of their bodies forced me back and with one wild, despairing grab I clutched the collar of the man nearest me and went over backward into the water.

Down, down I went, the man struggling wildly, first to strike at me, and then only to break free. Somehow, I'd caught a breath before I went under and, even as I fought my way to the surface, I held him down. I shook the water from my hair, gasped for breath and saw the flash of a gun. Something rapped my skull and down I went again.

Desperately, I floundered and got my head above water. I was some distance down-stream, trying to swim and breathe and clear my eyes.

My skull bursting with pain. Something huge and black loomed over me and I felt it closing in on me, huge, black and silent, and then something cold, something that bit at my hide. There was a momentary stab of pain, and blackness closed over me.

THE MOTION WAS EASY. Sunlight lay across my bunk, across the Indian blanket on which my hands lay. I could see my hands, and the slow movement of light that was one with the gentle motion.

For a long time I just lay and watched the light move toward my hands, touch them and then slowly move away. The rhythm was hypnotic. I watched it, dully conscious of my comfort, aware of nothing.

Something bumped near me and my eyes moved. They moved of their own volition, for there was no will. Now they were looking at the source of the light.

A round hole in the wall . . . a port-hole, I heard another dull thump, then a voice, "Still alive?"

"He's alive." It was a girl's voice. "Still unconscious I reckon. His pulse seemed stronger, though. We shouldn't have taken him from St. Louis, Pa. He might have had kin-folk nearby."

"Doubt it. Although he was dressed rich, some folks surely tried to kill him."

The talk came through the open port, but it meant nothing to me. I simply lay still, and my eyes had returned to the light on my hands.

Then I smelled something. It was a good smell, a rich smell . . . the smell of cooking.

My eyes blinked, my muscles stirred, and I hitched myself up in the bunk. My head was near the deck now and I could hear movements. Slowly, awareness came to me. I was in a clean, well-blanketed bunk, on some kind of a boat. Not a very big boat for the deck was right above my head and the bottom of the boat was right below me.

There was another bunk with a curtain in front of it. That was across the boat. There was a rack with some guns in it, and a small cubby-hole, where cooking was apparently done. There was a small table with a mirror behind it between the two bunks and against what was apparently the front of the boat.

I moved my legs, looked under the blanket. I was dressed in a homespun shirt and wore trousers cut off at the knee and tied with many folds around my waist with a knotted rope. The clothes were both too short and too wide to fit well. What boat was this, and where was I? Who was I? I considered that for a minute and then said aloud, "Jean Daniel Talon."

A voice exclaimed, and the curtain over the door drew back.

A girl stood there, a very small girl with a very petite figure, dark hair and eyes, very serious eyes now, and parted lips. She was pretty, very pretty.

She wore a fringed buckskin skirt and a calico blouse. She had moccasins on her feet.

"You're awake!"

"Either that, or you're a dream," I said.

She blushed. "You're awake," she said dryly. "Now you're hungry, no?"

"Now I am hungry . . . yes," I said. "But first, tell me where I am, what boat this is, and who you are."

"You're on the Kansas River about two miles up from the Missouri. This is my father's keel-boat, and I am my father's daughter."

"How did I get here? What happened?"

"You were hit on the head several times. Two cuts, many abrasions and scratches. You were shot . . . a furrow through your scalp. You can part your hair in the middle now, if you like."

"How did you save me?"

"We were coming up river, not stopping at St. Louis. We heard some yells, and a shot and then we saw a bunch of men on the end of a boat and about that time we saw you in the water. We were between you and them, so I reached over and grabbed you by the collar.

"Pa kept going, and I held on. Those men watched us and if we'd stopped to haul you aboard, they'd have been after us. So we just went on by, me hanging on to your collar until we got off into the night. We hit a straight stretch of river and Pa lashed the rudder. He come over and helped me pull you in."

"That was last night?"

"That was a week ago, come supper-time . . . or a mite later."

"A week!

"You saved my life, and for that I thank you, and I thank your father."

She canted her head on one side and looked at me. "You are hungry now? I have fed you many times . . . you don't remember?"

I was beginning to recall having awoken before. The memory of food made me even more hungry.

"I am ravenous. I could eat you."

She made a face. "I am not edible. Nor would my father like it. I am his crew."

"You? You're too small!"

"I am *not*!" She stuck out her chest. It was a very nice chest. "I am strong! I am formidable!"

"And I am hungry. Have we decided upon that?"

"Oh! I'm sorry. At once!"

I put my head back on the pillow and looked up at the under-pinning of the deck. It was good work . . . done with nails, of course. I prefer pegs and fitted joints. Nails . . . well, they are a convenience, but for fine work—

There were heavy steps on the deck and a man came down the ladder and then stopped, peering at me.

"Huh! You do not look so bad awake," he said. "What are you?"

I rolled up to my elbow. "A hungry man waiting for a meal. I am also a man who was banged about on the head. It still aches."

He chuckled. "You have some stitches. My daughter, she sews well, huh?"

"She stitched up my head?"

"What would you have us do? Leave flesh and hair over your ears? But no . . . it was not so bad. But some stitches were needed. They will come out some day. Do not worry."

"How far are we from St. Louis?"

He shrugged. "Far is a question always? How far? On foot? By keel-boat? By horse? And how much of a hurry is it?"

"I left some people there, and I want to pick up some guns."

"You are in no shape to ride. Even if you had a horse."

"I have horses in St. Louis."

He shrugged. "Maybe you have a castle on the moon.

Both of them are far away, and I am not going back to St. Louis."

"You are not one of Choteau's people?"

"I? I am my own people. We have this boat Yvette and I. It is our boat. We have some traps. We catch a few fish. We pick berries along the river, and we know where they grow. Sometimes we shoot a buffalo or an antelope or deer. We sell our furs. We are nobody's people."

"Yvette . . . it is a pretty name."

"It is. It was her mother's name, God rest her soul. But do not throw sheep's eyes at my daughter. She is my crew. Without her, I am nothing. Without her I am an old man with an empty boat."

"You are far from old."

"The day she leaves me, that little one, I am old. I shall be old upon the minute."

He walked over and sat down opposite me. He was nearly as broad as he was tall, with wide, thick shoulders, and no fat. He had square, powerful hands.

"You tell me now, while she is busy. What was it about?"

"They were trying to kill me. Not to rob me, to kill me."

He brushed that away. "Certainly. I can see that."

"There is a steamboat on the river, a steamboat that looks like a great black serpent."

"I have seen it."

"It is owned by a girl, a very lovely girl named Tabitha Majoribanks. She has come west looking for her brother, Charles. She has a man for captain named Macklem. It was his men who attacked me."

"She does not like you . . . this woman?"

"It is not the woman. It is Macklem and a man named Torville, a very dangerous man. Macklem is joining some other men somewhere up the Missouri. They wish to take it all, this Louisiana Territory."

He took out his pipe and began to tamp tobacco into the bowl. "You are ten years behind the times. This is no longer Louisiana. It is now the Missouri Territory." He paused. "He would take it, huh? He has something to do, that one."

"Nevertheless, he will try."

He looked at me thoughtfully. "You are in love with this woman?"

"No!" I spoke quickly, perhaps too quickly, for he looked amused. "I would help her find her brother, but also it is to defeat this man that I am here."

"Macklem?"

"Him, too. I apologize, it is complicated and I'm still collecting my wits."

"And you have met this Torville?"

"No."

"Then I have the advantage. I know him." He put the pipe in his mouth and touched a match to it. "I also know the young Charles. A good boy. A very good boy."

CHAPTER XVIII

WE TIED UP near a rocky creek and talked into the dark hours. Yvette fed us, then made coffee, and made coffee again. LeBrun, who was her father, was an easy man. He was quick to see, to understand.

He had met Torville on his first journey into the Mississippi Valley, and did not like him. He had also met Charles Majoribanks when he was with the Yellowstone expedition. Charles did not have an official position, merely that of friendship with several of those aboard, and they had made room for him. After all, he was a fine botanist and eager to be involved.

"Where is he now?"

"Who knows? He went up the river, and did not come back." He paused, lighting his pipe again. "We go to find him."

"On the Kansas?"

LeBrun shrugged. "To travel by day on the Missouri is not always safe, my friend. As you have said, there are men about who are dangerous. I am a man alone, with a young daughter. So we will travel west a short ways and see what we hear from any Indians or returning trappers we meet. If we must backtrack, so be it . . . but until we know what we are up against it is best to stay off the Missouri."

Slowly, I eased to my feet and attempted to stand up.

Yvette watched anxiously; her father simply watched. He knew what I was feeling, knew that a man has things to be done that cannot be done lying on his back in bed.

Shakily, I got to my feet, my head spinning. I tried a step, staggered, caught myself as Yvette started quickly forward, and then slowly sat down again.

"You need rest!" she protested.

"You've been looking for Charles," I said. "Why?"

Yvette flushed a little, then put her chin up. "We like him."

"It is reason enough," I said. "And nothing else?"

"What more is necessary?" LeBrun asked. "He was a good companion. He talked of flowers and trees, of their need for each other, and how the value of the soil may be judged by the plants."

"He liked my cooking, too," Yvette said.

"I have no doubt that was not all he liked. Even a botanist can have eyes for more than plants."

She blushed. "He was a nice man, a gentleman."

"You have no horse?" I asked LeBrun. I had seen keelboats that carried draft horses to pull the boat along canals and well-travelled waterways.

"Out here? No, that would just tempt the Indians."

"I must have a horse. I must go first to St. Louis to my friends, and to get my outfit."

"Well," LeBrun rubbed his jaw thoughtfully. "There's some Omahas over east of here a mite. They're good folks, mostly, and we set well with them. Might make us a trade."

"And what have I to trade? I'm thankful for being alive but this is a disaster!"

"You got your clothes," he said, "and you've got a mighty fine pistol, and a knife like I never seen."

"I can trade the clothes, and the pistol . . . not the knife. It has been in my family for around two hundred years."

It was pleasant talking with them, but I was suddenly very tired. I lay back on the bunk and looked up at the deck overhead. Too bad they had to use nails. Those were good timbers, well cut and trimmed, they could have—

When I awakened again it was dark and still. I lay very quiet, suddenly alert and listening. There was no sound but a faint creaking of timbers.

It was too silent.

No breathing came from the opposite bed, now hidden behind a curtain. Very gently I eased back the blankets and put my feet to the floor, feeling for my moccasins. One hand reached for the pistol, drawing it near. Stepping into my pants I drew them up, drawing the rope that was my belt tight, listening all the while. I had the faintest memories of the boat scraping bottom, of a sense of it being caught by the current. This must have happened just as I awoke.

Still no sound but the faint lap of water. There was a vague sense of the keel-boat moving, drifting back down river. I moved to the steps that led to the deck, if such it could be called.

A keel-boat of the smaller size, which this was, was usually about forty feet along, and eight or nine feet wide, with both bow and stern pointed. The deck-house occupied more than half the length with a steering pulpit aft and seats forward for oar men. One square-sail was mounted atop the forward part of the deck-house.

Along each side was a cleated walk used by polers in working the boat up-stream. Obviously, with only Yvette and himself aboard, LeBrun must depend on the sail for going up-stream, the current when going down.

Stepping out to the narrow walkway, I crouched to keep my head below the level of the deck-house. For a moment I held perfectly still, listening.

The water rippled, the sensation of movement was more pronounced . . . we were adrift.

I looked aft toward the steering pulpit where LeBrun should be. No figure loomed against the night.

Very cautiously, I worked my way aft, crouching when I reached the after end of the deck-house. The small deck in the stern was empty.

Staying low behind the bulwarks I reached the rudder. The proper steering position was from the pulpit but I'd no intention of sky-lining myself up there, so I raised a hand to the handle and gently centered it.

Where were LeBrun and Yvette? And who had set the boat adrift?

There was no doubt in my mind that it had been deliberately set adrift, but why I could not guess.

Indians? I doubted it. They would have been more inclined to come aboard and loot the boat.

Keeping my left hand on the rudder, I managed to keep the boat away from the banks. From my crouching position, or even standing and merging my body with the rudder-post I could not see the river ahead. Fortunately, the Kansas this close to the Missouri was probably free of obstructions, and I prayed that it was.

There had to be some reason for setting the boat adrift. Had LeBrun and Yvette gone ashore for some reason, offering unseen enemies a chance to get me out of the picture? Or . . . and this was more likely, did someone simply wish to keep LeBrun from returning to the protection offered by the boat?

If that was true they were, no doubt, closing in on LeBrun, wherever he was. So, what to do?

Although I'd had no experience with keel-boats I realized that if I turned into the bank and failed to ground her, the current might swing me around with the stern down-stream, making the boat fairly unmanageable.

Feeling sure my idea was correct, I crawled into the pulpit where I could see the river ahead and get a better grip on the rudder. For a moment I gripped the rudder, expecting a bullet at any moment . . . but none came.

I guided the boat closer to the bank, watching for a place where I might run it in close and tie up. At all costs, I must get back to our campsite.

The river took a slight bend and there was a sort of a notch where the mouth of a creek entered. Leaning on the rudder I headed in close to the bank, grounded the bow, then leaped ashore with a line. I took a quick turn around a sturdy tree, then another turn and a half-hitch and still another.

Climbing back aboard I went quickly to the bulkhead where I'd seen a rifle.

It was gone.

In the pocket of my coat I found several lead balls for my pistol and I took a powder-horn that hung where the rifle had been and a wad of grease-soaked patches. I laced tight a pair of moccasins that were too big for my feet then over the side I went, and into the woods. How far had we drifted? A mile? I doubted it. Likely less than half of that distance.

I started to run. Running had been a means of travel for me for years. In the eastern woods neither Indian nor white man had many horses, and to travel for miles through the woods at a swinging trot was the usual means of travel. My head hurt and my gait was unsteady, but I kept at it. Suddenly, I saw a gleam on the water, the ripple of a familiar-looking creek and a water-soaked length of heavy rope. I stopped.

All was very still. I moved forward on cat feet, pausing at every other step to listen. Finally, near the trunk of a huge old tree, I crouched down. Where were LeBrun and his daughter?

Easing forward to another tree, I paused again. My feet, through the soles of the moccasins, sensed some change in the earth beneath. No leaves, no grass. I bent over and felt the ground.

Hard-packed earth . . . only a few inches wide, but long.

A path. A path from the river to—?

For a moment I listened, then I carefully followed the path. When I had gone no more than two hundred yards, I heard a faint sound.

Drawing back I dropped to one knee near a bush. Someone was coming!

At the same moment I became aware that I was not alone. Not more than six feet away, I could faintly see the outline of a head and the whiteness of a face, a man was crouched and waiting.

The man shifted around nervously. "Newt? You hear somethin' a moment ago?"

"Ssh!"

"Newt, I—"

"Ssh damn it! They're comin'."

Now I could sense where the other man, Newt, was. I caught some movement as he turned his head slightly and could make out the faint gleam of his face. He was crouched just ahead of the first man I'd spotted.

Rising up only slightly, I took a careful step forward. The night was cool and still. I could see both of them more clearly now. I put my hand on the cold barrel of my pistol, chilling my fingertips.

Somebody was coming. I heard a faint murmur of voices, talking very low. My fingers cold from the gun barrel, I reached out and touched the bare neck of the man before me.

He leaped like a startled rabbit. "A-a-agh!" he gave out with a choking scream and crashed into the man ahead of him who swore and smashed wildly backward with his gun butt. It missed, and his accomplice leaped into the brush thrashing away down the creek.

Newt stumbled forward swearing viciously and trying to peer through the darkness.

"Lookin' for something, Newt?" I asked very softly.

He had nerve, I'll give him credit. He leaped right at my voice. I'd no desire to shoot, not knowing where LeBrun and Yvette might be hiding, so I stiff-armed him in the face with the butt of my palm, then clubbed my pistol-barrel over his skull. He dropped in his tracks.

Squatting beside him, I took his gun and knife. The gun I slid behind my belt, the knife I tossed into the brush, and then I felt around for his rifle, sure there would be one. The moment I put my hand on it I knew from the shape and weight that it was a trade-musket of the kind sold to the Indians.

I stood up. "It is all right," I said quietly. "One's down and the other one's still running."

Yvette and LeBrun came along the trail then, and I stepped out where they could see me. "They cut the boat loose," I said, "but I tied her up down-stream a ways. Shall we get along down there?"

"What about him? Is he dead?"

"Doubt it. He's too hard-headed. Let's take him along. Maybe he can tell us something."

LeBrun handed off his rifle and what looked like the haunch of an antelope or small deer to Yvette and caught the unconscious man by the scruff of the neck and jerked him erect. The fellow moved, seemed to be conscious.

"Walk!" LeBrun commanded. "Or *I'll* hit you!"

The man stumbled along, gradually gaining more command of his feet. When we were aboard the keel-boat we took in the line and drifted down-stream to the confluence of the Missouri. Laying alongside a brush-choked sand-bar, we tied up again.

With heavy canvas curtains over the port-holes, LeBrun lighted a lamp.

The man was a stranger, a surly-looking fellow with a streak of blood from a broken scalp to add to the dirt and whiskers on his face.

"Your friend's still running," I said, grinning at him. "I just touched him on the back of the neck with a cold hand. Jumped right out of his skin."

"Yeller!" the be-whiskered man sneered. "Yeller clean through. I told Baker he was no good."

Baker . . . that was one name.

"What d' you want them for?" I asked, gesturing toward LeBrun and Yvette.

"None o' yer damn business!!" he snapped, and I slapped him across the mouth.

Like I've said, I've a heavy hand. It smashed his head around on his neck and jolted him to his heels, although to my notion it had not been a hard slap.

"I don't like that sort of talk," I said mildly. Yvette had started forward and was staring at me, wide-eyed.

"I like the kind of talk that has information," I said calmly. "I want to know who everybody is, where everybody is, and what they're planning to do."

He started to make an angry reply and I lifted my hand. He shrank away, and I could see he had no particular taste for it. "Do you no good," he said. "He'll kill you, anyway. Them too," he glanced at LeBrun. "They been too noisy. That's what he told me . . . 'Kill 'em,' says he, 'I don't want to be bothered.' 'What about the girl?' I says, an' him he just shrugs. 'Just so she doesn't talk,' he says."

"Who is it you're talking about?" I asked.

"None o' yer—" I lifted my hand, and he shrugged. "Do y' no good, anyway. Yer dead. Yer dead as a doornail. He'll see to that. I mean the Baron."

"Torville?"

"Who else? He's got him a thousand white men and three thousand Injuns. They're set up in camps all along the river. He's goin' to take them sojers first and then the rest o' you as he moves. We're goin' to *own* this country. Right from St. Louis to Santy Fe, you'll see."

"Where is he?" I demanded.

Suddenly a rush of water rocked the boat and we heard the low chug-chug of an engine.

"That's him now," the man said, "an' he's got y' dead to rights!"

CHAPTER XIX

WITH A GUN barrel against the man's back, I blew out the light. There was some moonlight outside, but we lay close under the bank with branches hanging around us. Unless we had been seen there was every chance we might be passed by.

Peering out of the port I saw it. Huge, black and glistening, the great eyes of the serpent staring ahead, the smoke puffing from the flared nostrils, the fins obscuring any sight of the stern-wheel that churned the water behind it.

It was, I had to admit, a fearsome object. Whether it had ever frightened Indians I had no idea, but it did give off a sense of enormous power, of evil, and mystery.

"Long's Dragon. I've seen her before," LeBrun said, "she mounts a fair number of cannon."

"That's right," our prisoner growled. "We could destroy St. Louis!"

"What are they doing?" Yvette asked.

"Passing by." As the man was looking toward the port, I nudged LeBrun. "Which way did those Indians go?"

"Injuns?" The prisoner turned his head sharply. "Here?"

"We've been seeing war parties all day," I said quietly. "That's why we hid the boat."

An idea was already working itself around in my head

and we had no time to watch over a prisoner. I wanted him away from us, not knowing what we were doing, but frightened enough to be cautious as to trying to signal the serpent ship.

"Worries me," LeBrun said. "They were from up river and they looked to be scalp-hunting. I know some o' them, but when they're huntin' scalps they'll take what they find."

"Gives me an idea," I said, "let's just turn this man loose."

The prisoner's head came around sharply.

"Let's leave him ashore. He'll get back to his friends if he's lucky, but if the Indians need a scalp, they can take his."

"Now, see here," the man protested.

"Get him ashore," I told LeBrun.

Despite the man's protests, we put him ashore. "If I were you," I said, low-voiced, "I'd be almighty quiet. You be quiet and you might get up-stream to where your outfit is. We've got no time to watch over you and the girl doesn't want you killed. Lucky for you she's soft-hearted or we'd just tie you to a tree and see how long it took them to find you."

He was gone into the brush and we got back aboard. "Cast off," I said. "Now that we know they are ahead of us, let's get out of here."

"There's a breeze coming up," LeBrun said, "we might make some time up-stream before daylight."

"Try it then," I said.

With poles we pushed off. The keel-boat got into the current and we slipped away down-stream. We finally got out of the full sweep of the current losing scarcely a half-mile in the process. We got our sail up and the keel-boat began edging up the Missouri, with painful slowness. The steamboat could easily do five or six miles an hour against the stream, while we would be lucky to do one.

When I took the rudder and LeBrun went below for coffee, I was alone with Yvette. "You said you were going to find Charles . . . do you know where he is?"

"We think we do."

"You believe he is in trouble?"

"Yes . . . when they can use him no longer, they will kill him. I think he knows this."

"He cannot escape?"

"How? There are many men with Torville. They would track him down and have him at once, and then they would kill him. We must get him to the river to get away."

"With that steamboat? It can travel much faster than you."

"Maybe. Papa does not think their pilot is good, and the pilot *must* be good. There are snags, sand-bars and sawyers—"

"What's a sawyer?"

"A tree whose roots or branches are buried in the mud at the bottom. It bobs up and down, swings back and forth with the current. One of them can take the bottom right out of a boat. Papa knows the river. He has been on it many times in keel-boats and canoes. He says there is no river like it and he has worked on the Ohio, the St. Lawrence and the Mississippi."

THE WIND HELD strong and we moved along, gaining a little speed. The banks were low, thick with trees and brush. In the moonlight the channel was clear, but the current was strong.

Suddenly, I caught sight of something on the water, just ahead. "Yvette?" I whispered, for sound carries easily over water. "What is it?"

She ran forward, yet in a moment she was back. "It's a canoe. There are three men in it."

With our sail we were gaining, but not very much. LeBrun came out and stood by the rail, rifle in hand. My own pistol was behind my belt, the butt easily reached,

"They're waiting for us," Yvette said suddenly. "They're paddling just enough to keep going."

It was true, and suddenly a low voice called out, "Ahoy, there! Stand by!"

The voice was one not easy to forget. It was Jambe-de-Bois.

"It's all right, LeBrun," I said. "I know one of them."

"Yvette, take the rudder. Come over here, Talon."

His rifle covered them. "Stand by," he said quietly. "You know *one* of them. We do not know the others." He glanced at me again. "How well do you know the one?"

"Well enough."

"Talon?" I knew that voice, too. "This is McQuarrie. Can we board you?"

I nodded to LeBrun and he lowered his weapon. I passed them a line to which they made fast the canoe, and pulled them in close. McQuarrie scrambled aboard, then Jambe-de-Bois. For all his peg-leg he came up nimbly enough. No doubt he had boarded many a craft in his day.

The third man then came up, and he was a stranger. A stocky, well set-up man in buckskins. A mountain man by the look of him.

"Have you seen the black ship?" McQuarrie asked.

"Aye," I said. "She went up the river back there, skimmed right past us, and lucky for us she did."

"Who are these men?" LeBrun demanded.

Explanations required only a few minutes.

LeBrun glanced at the sail. It was bellied out and the keel-boat was moving well, despite the current. "Hold to the channel," he said to Yvette. "We'll be up in a minute."

He led the way below, then turned to look at first one and then the other. "Where is it you're bound?"

"I was huntin' him," Jambe-de-Bois said, indicating me.

"Hunting him? How could you know he was alive?"

"I knew nothing, only there was talk of a big fight and I found his hat on the wharf, so I asked around and some said there was a boat passing at the time. Thinks I, with his luck, he got aboard of her. The dragon boat was headed this way so it seemed the thing to do."

"And you?"

McQuarrie shrugged. "I am a British officer. I understand I have no authority here, but I want Torville. He is a murderer and a traitor."

The buckskin clad man shrugged. "I am Otis Pinkney. I think you know of me."

LeBrun nodded. "Indeed I do. And you're welcome aboard. Make yourselves at home here. It will be dawn soon and we'll have a hole to hunt."

There was coffee in the pot, and we shared it, there was beef jerky, and we tried that.

McQuarrie indicated Pinkney with a bob of his head. "He brought news."

"I did," Pinkney said. "Two mackinaw boats, loaded with furs, gone from the river. Six men gone with them, and five bodies found, scalped."

"Furs worth at least thirty thousand dollars," McQuarrie added, "and the one man missing may be alive."

"You mean he was a traitor?"

"We think so. His name was none too good on the river. They call him Bill Pastor . . . there was no sign of him after the fight, but he'd started down river with them."

"I've somethin' for you," Jambe-de-Bois grinned. "Choteau sent it."

"How'd he know I was alive?"

Jambe-de-Bois grinned. "I lied, I told him you sent me for them . . . the guns, I mean." He opened a sack and took out the Pally rifle and the Collier pistols. "Figured if you were dead, I'd just hang on to them. Your pack and tools are in the canoe."

I took the rifle in my hands. It was what I had wanted. A good, fast-shooting gun. And the pistols. There were pouches of ammunition for each of them as well as tools for cleaning and the casting of balls.

Yvette came to the door. "We will tie up now. Papa needs help."

It was already vaguely light. In the middle of the river was a large sand-bar on which grew clumps of brush among the piled up driftwood. We slipped past and then behind an island, an island covered with willows and a thick growth of underbrush and wild plum trees. There, in a position that hid all sight of the keel-boat, we tied up to a huge old tree that had beached itself on the island and become half-buried in the sand.

We all were tired. Leaving the cabin to Yvette and LeBrun, the rest of us stretched out on deck.

When I awakened some hours later, the sun was high and all was quiet. The others were still asleep. Dressing in my own clothes and belting on my two new pistols, I stuck Foulsham's in my pocket, took the rifle and went ashore. I wandered along the edge of the island, close to the brush searching for a spot to have a look up river. There were wild grapes in profusion, and many wild raspberries. Pausing here and there to eat, I also listened for any sound, any movement.

Somehow we must locate Charles Majoribanks and free him . . . if he was a prisoner, as we assumed. Next, we must locate the dragon ship and keep it under observation. If Tabitha was no longer in command, we must somehow capture the steamboat and take her back down to St. Louis. In the process, we needed to somehow disrupt whatever plans Torville and Macklem had.

The late morning was very still and overcast but with clouds that might disappear by noon. Again, I paused. The willows were very thick where I stood. Looking through the leaves I could see several deer at the edge of the water, drinking.

Suddenly, the head of one doe came up, then the others. Instantly, I was alert. Waiting, listening, I heard the faint sound of a paddle in the water, and then a canoe. In it were four Indians, a man, two women and a young boy.

They came in close and the man held the bow in to the sandy shore while the boy sprang ashore and tugged it up onto the sand. The others then came ashore and hauled the canoe higher.

Obviously, they were a family on the move. I walked out from the willows toward them and they saw me at once, standing very still, all eyes on me. I held my hand up in a sign of peace, and spoke to them. "You have come far?"

The man hesitated, then spoke slowly, "Far."

They wore moccasins of elk skin blackened with smoke, with an ornamental seam across the back and flaps turned outward. It was little enough I knew about western Indians, but this I had learned from Butlin, that such moccasins were worn by the Omaha.

I gestured toward the brush. "Many berries . . . good." I rubbed my stomach and grinned at them, showing the few I had in my hand.

The women had gone about making a fire. They had chosen a spot sheltered from the main stream of the river by a clump of chokecherry brush.

"You hunt?" I asked the man.

He gestured up-stream. "Much hunt. Buffalo. You see?"

"Not yet." I gestured toward the brush behind me. "My boat is there. Many men. We look for a man." I described Charles, as he had been described to me "Maybe with bad man . . . bad white man," I added.

He squatted down and lit a pipe.

"Big serpent boat. You know?"

"Black," he said, "I know."

"You be careful," I suggested, "some good men, some bad men with it."

"Bad men," he looked at me gravely, but his eyes twinkled, "make big snake work hard. Carry steamboat on back."

His name, he told me, was Red Tail, and he was going with his family to visit an Otoe village that lay on a river I took to be the Kansas.

"Long time ago," he said, puffing on his pipe, "Omahas big people . . . big nation. Much sickness . . . many attacks by the Sioux. We are few now . . . maybe ninety warriors.

"It is no longer as it was," he said, the words coming to him as he spoke, "the old ways are gone. One time we teach young boys how to be warrior, how to be man. We teach with the making of the arrow, now they no longer listen, the gun is big medicine."

"It is easier now, with the white man's pots? Easier to boil food? Easier to hunt with his gun?" I asked.

He looked at me. "Easy not good," he said bluntly. "One time Omaha stalk deer . . . come close before shoot. Stalk very good. Now shoot from way off . . . no stalk so good. Omaha forget old ways."

"It is so with us, too," I said, "the old ways change. I, too, think the easy is not always good. It is better to do what makes a man strong."

He nodded, then he said, "It is our name . . . we Omaha are those who go against the wind. Long ago we built our lodges on the Wabash, but there is much trouble and we move west. Our friends, the Quapaw, they go down the river . . . we go up, sometimes to where the red stone is found to make pipes . . . we go with the Ponca, but there was much fighting and the Dakota are stronger, and now we are here."

I got to my feet. "I go back to my people, Red Tail." I held out my hand. "May there always be meat in your lodge."

He chuckled. "Always meat . . . I get fat behind and slow in the head." He was still chuckling as he walked back to the others.

Walking swiftly, I returned to the keel-boat. Rather, I returned to where I expected it to be. It was gone.

CHAPTER XX

GONE!

I came out of the willows and looked around, unwilling to believe the boat was not there.

My tracks were still upon the sand, and others as well. Looking carefully about, I then went forward.

There was scuffed sand . . . running feet, no doubt. The line tying up the keel-boat had again been cut. A few feet of rope was still tied to the tree and trailed off into the water.

Up-stream or down? It had to be up, for otherwise I would have seen the boat in the distance from where I had been talking to Red Tail.

Turning swiftly, I ran back through the willows, slowing only when I drew near the camp, but they had heard me coming, and Red Tail and his son were on their feet.

It needed a solid half-hour of bargaining, and I was lucky at that, but I traded Foulsham's pistol and my shirt for Red Tail's canoe.

He would of course make another one before leaving the spot, giving his son a valuable lesson in the meantime. Once the trade was made I wasted no time. I had always been good with a canoe, since childhood when I paddled to Perce Rock and Bonaventure Island.

Now, with my rifle close beside me I started up-stream, holding to the slack water closer to the banks to avoid the main current. They could be no more than an hour ahead of me, yet I had no wish to come up to them before darkness.

Somebody had captured the keel-boat and all aboard. I had seen no blood, no bodies.

I dipped the paddle deep and the canoe shot forward. For that mile, with swift, sure strokes, I went up-stream at a rate that would have won many a race, but I had always loved a canoe, and this one was light and finely made. Red Tail was an artist, if the work was his.

Skirting the river's next bend I went by an inside route the larger boat could not have taken, for there were only inches of water beneath my keel, yet the short-cut saved me several hundred yards.

Rounding the next small bend, I kept an island between me and the river ahead. Now I settled down to a slower, more even pace, dodging among the low islands. Three hours of steady paddling passed before I caught a glimpse of the mast beyond some trees.

Checking my rifle, I eased off, glided into a narrow run of water between two brush-covered sand-bars. I slipped up river with slow, even strokes.

The keel-boat was a good mile and a half ahead, and had only a small breeze, just enough to keep it moving. The sun was going down but an hour of light remained, perhaps a bit more.

Near the end of a small island I turned in. There was no more cover and I must not be seen. Drawing the canoe up on the shore, I looked hastily around. I was alone. Running low I got to where I could look across the island and on to the main channel. Stretching out on the sand, I let the keel-boat draw away from me. I tried to see who was steering, but could make out nothing at the distance. At last, it disappeared.

Getting to my feet I returned to the canoe, put my rifle against the thwart once more, and shoved off. Now I need not hurry. The keel-boat was before me and my time would come.

The last light was slipping away, the banks were casting dark shadows, and here and there a huge old tree leaned above the river like some monstrous hand, waiting to grab whatever came near.

I felt good. The paddling exhilarated me, and I felt prepared for anything. My coat had been left aboard the keel-boat, and I had traded my shirt, so I was naked to the waist. The night-wind felt cool and good.

For some time I had been dimly conscious of a peculiar sound. It was a dull murmur, something I could not place.

Rapids? A water-fall?

Then it dawned upon me. It was a steam engine, its sound merging with the churning of the current. I dug my paddle deep and turned toward the shadows of the shore. Narrowly missing a huge sawyer, I angled across, glimpsing a barely submerged sand-bar. I skirted it, then crossed over.

The sound was unmistakable now. The steamer was behind me, coming up-stream. Had it tied up to release a scouting party? The scouting party that had discovered the keel-boat? Had it stopped to cut wood, been grounded or otherwise delayed and we had slipped past it? The river was a maze of channels; there was no way to be sure.

Easing with my paddle, I slid into the brushy background of the bank. I watched the serpent ship come steaming up the river. Huge, black, glistening with spray, the great flared nostrils puffing smoke and occasional sparks, it came on.

Tabitha was aboard there, Macaire and probably Butlin. And Macklem, of course. Lights gleamed from portholes, and the *Western Engineer* passed with a great churning of water from the stern-wheel. As it passed, I moved out from the shore and started forward.

Catching the steamer would be impossible now until they came up to the keel-boat. I was tired, but I kept moving, dipping my paddle in a sort of dull, hypnotic movement that carried me forward. I skirted a high bank, lost some distance in the current, then escaped from it. And then I saw them silhouetted against the sky ahead of me . . . hove to, side by side.

Under cover of darkness, I moved slowly forward. They were not only side by side, they were in trouble. The keel-boat seemed to be trapped in a sort of cul-de-sac in a sand-bar, but the steamer, trying to come alongside, had run hard and fast aground.

I had a hunch that the whole thing was intentional, that LeBrun, who knew the river as well as any man, seeing the steamboat coming up had deliberately moved right up to the sand-bar instead of skirting it. Prisoner he might be, but he had managed to be at the rudder when the time came. No doubt his captors were willing enough to let him work.

The sand-bar was a few inches under water, and in fact my canoe glided right over it. Gently, to make no sound, I moved closer, tying up to a nearby snag.

Then I waited, and listened.

My position was no more than thirty yards off the stern of the keel-boat, between it and the shore. Resting in the canoe I could hear some stirring around onboard.

Suddenly a commanding voice called out from the steamboat, "Baker? Is Talon aboard there?"

"No, he's not. There's the peg-leg, LeBrun and LeBrun's girl, but there's no Talon."

"Just the three of them?"

"There's a Britisher . . . at least he sounds it. Says his name is McQuarrie."

"Ah?" There was cruel satisfaction in Macklem's tone. "So I've got another one of them, have I?"

That accounted for them all but Pinkney. There was no mention of him.

"Stand by then, Baker, and look sharp. As soon as we float this ship we'll pick you all up. Get a line rigged to tie on. We'll tow you up-stream."

Something stirred in the water near me. It was no time for shooting, I drew my knife, and held it low, with a cutting edge up.

The steamer's engines began to turn over and the great stern-wheel threshed madly at the water, in reverse. There was no movement.

My eyes remained away from the steamboat, waiting for whatever it was that was closing in.

Then, during a lull in the frantic efforts of the steamer to dislodge itself, a low voice spoke, "Talon? Pinkney here."

"Come in slow," I said, "I've got knife enough to float your guts on the river."

He waded over, hands up, rifle aloft. It was him, all

right. Nimbly, he slipped into the canoe and I sheathed my blade.

"Well, there they are, lad," he said, calling me lad and him not more than four or five years older. Well, a little older than that. "We've got our work laid out for us. What had you in mind?"

"To take the steamer. Are any of ours hurt?"

"LeBrun took a rap on the skull. I saw it was no use and ducked behind the cargo for'rd. When the chance came, I went over the side."

I explained what had happened to me. He leaned over and, whispering so softly it was almost lost in the rustle of water, asked, "On the steamer? Is there anyone?"

"There's Macaire, he's a good man. And I think there's a man aboard there as a hand . . . name of Butlin."

"You don't say? Ol' Calgary there?" he chuckled. "That shines. I know him . . . know him well. We trapped a winter on Lake o' the Woods, far to the north. Got hisself clawed by a cross bear. She raked him down the back and ripped his pants to the hide. After that we called him 'Bear' Butlin."

He was quiet for a moment. "That's something to remember. Nobody but the three or four of us who knew him then would know that story. Might be a way of him knowin' there was friends about."

How that would work, I had no idea. To make any kind of sound would give away our presence and at the moment we were but two able and free men.

"We've got to take the keel-boat," I whispered, "free McQuarrie, Jambe-de-Bois and LeBrun. Five is better than two. How many does he have aboard, d' you think?"

"Twenty-five or thirty."

"Let's go," I was suddenly through talking. "Let's go now."

He pulled the slip-knot and I dug in the paddle and we moved away from the snag and toward the keel-boat. We had made two lengths when somebody moving along the side-deck saw us.

He stopped abruptly. "Hey? Who's there?" The man inhaled sharply, then pitched from the side into the water. There was a loud splash and Otis Pinkney said, "Move in close to him, lad, I want to get my knife back."

"Your knife? What in—?"

"Not bad, for the distance and the dark," Pinkney said complacently, "of course, we were moving in on him all the while."

We bumped the side and I took a turn around a kevel, then threw a couple of quick half-hitches. Pinkney was already aboard, rifle in his hand, knife in his teeth.

I followed.

Two men were coming toward me. "Get below and turn 'em loose," I told Otis, and moved in fast. They weren't expecting trouble until one of them started to speak and I swung the Pauly rifle butt around with my left hand. It caught him alongside the head with a solid *thunk* and he hit the deck. The second man was no yellow-belly. He came at me.

He was already in close, so I brought my fist up in a good stiff uppercut and his head snapped back like it was on a hinge. His feet left the deck and he hit the boards in a sitting position. It was no time for polite work, and I swung a neat kick to his chin and went on across him toward the others who were coming.

Somebody on the steamer yelled, "What's goin' on over there?"

Four men were coming at me and I'd no time to reply, and I wanted to leave my shooting for later, so I put the rifle down on the deck-house as I scrambled over it heading for the bow and the four men. I went in swinging, and had the advantage of a good start. My first blow was a wild one but it caught a man coming in. He grunted, and then I was right in the middle of the wildest fist-swinging brawl I'd found in a coon's age.

There was four of them and the trouble was that they had to hunt a target and be careful not to hit each other, and all I had to do was punch. I rolled my shoulders up near my chin, and went in with short arm punches. Then when somebody grabbed at my head I took him by both legs and dumped him over the side. I back-handed another one with a blow that probably jarred his relatives wherever they were, and somebody clobbered me on the side of the head. Another one swung on my kidney, so I got my back into the V of the bow and they closed in on me. I ducked a punch, hitting hard with my right into his belly. He gasped like he'd been hit with a bath of cold water, and I swung him across in front of me and struck past his head at an open face. An open face that now had fewer teeth. It was a wild Brannigan. I was enjoying it, but there were too many and I knew I was in trouble. Then somebody closed in behind them. A body splashed in the water and then another. It was McQuarrie wielding a truncheon of some sort. LeBrun pushed past him with a bloody hatchet and began chopping at the tow line.

The keel-boat fell away and somebody fired a musket from the stern of the *Western Engineer*.

"The Hell with that!" It was Macklem shouting. "Sink 'em!"

And they had the cannon to do it.

"Get the sail up, damn it!" I yelled and scrambled to retrieve my rifle.

LeBrun and Otis were pushing off with poles, trying to get into the current, which was off to our port. We made it and the faster moving water carried us back.

We saw the flash of the gun and heard its boom almost together, and a shot splash aft of us. Then another flash and the starboard bulwark was torn through and splinters flew in every direction. Some small ones stung my face and, down on one knee, I aimed a little higher than where the flash had come from and squeezed off my shot.

Somebody yelled, but the gun flared as he must have had the match in his hand, and another shot struck us but struck at an angle and glanced off into the night.

We were falling away rapidly into the darkness when we got the sail up and the wind was blowing up-stream. It caught the sail, she steadied down and after a moment began to inch forward and across the stream. The steamer was off in the darkness, but suddenly her engines began to pound and the wheel to thresh.

"If he gets loose," it was McQuarrie beside me, "we're through."

We stood in silence staring off into the dark. We all knew what it meant. With steam they were faster, they could outmaneuver us, and we would be dead . . . all of us.

"We've got to go ashore," I said. "We've got to leave her."

"What's that?" LeBrun had come forward, leaving Yvette at the rudder. "Leave my boat?"

"It's a small choice. They'll shell it to bits. Leave it. We can strike out overland."

"His Indians will track us down," LeBrun objected.

"We'll have no chance if we stay aboard," I said.

He looked at me, angrily, but it was not me his anger was directed at. It was just the nature of things.

"There's a creek," he said, "it's shallow but partly hidden by an island."

There was still an hour before dawn when we left the keel-boat.

CHAPTER XXI

EACH OF US carried a small packet of food, a blanket, and whatever ammunition we had. Fortunately, Jambe-de-Bois had brought enough for my three guns, including the metal and paper-cartridges required for the Pauly.

We were a rough lot. With Otis Pinkney leading off, followed by LeBrun and Yvette, then McQuarrie, Jambe-de-Bois, and myself.

Pinkney led the way up a slight bank through the cottonwoods and out across a small meadow. That he had some destination in mind was obvious. He travelled fast, rarely looking back, his first intention was that of leaving the river as far behind as possible.

When we had travelled for an hour, he paused in a grove of huge old cottonwoods on a small branch that ran down toward the Missouri. There were a few wild plums, which we all ate, and we drank from the stream. He led off again after only a few minutes but at a somewhat slower pace, and we skirted the trees on the south side, staying away from the river.

FOR THREE DAYS we travelled steadily. Several times we saw buffalo, and on the second day I killed a cow and we divided the meat after eating what we could. We all made fresh moccasins from the hide. The green hide would not last as long as seasoned hide, but all of us had worn out our foot-gear.

We ate, then rested. All of us were on edge. Now that we were here, none of us had a very good idea of what we should do. If there were as many men as we'd heard, we would have no chance at making any sort of direct attack. To rescue Charles and Tabitha was the first order of business, yet throwing a kink in the plans of Torville appealed to me almost as much.

"There's only one thing to do," I said, at last. "We must capture the serpent."

"Supposin' your Miss Majoribanks isn't aboard?" LeBrun suggested.

The same thought had worried me. "We'll have to chance it," I said. "We will have to move in fast and quietly, take the boat, and then if Tabi—if Miss Majoribanks is ashore, we will have to go after her. Besides their numbers the boat is their primary asset. Stealing it will deal a blow to the plot and allow us to make our getaway."

At dusk we moved out. Shortly after we started we came upon the freshly killed carcass of a buffalo. It was still light enough to see heel marks and the tracks of shod horses.

We moved quietly, working our way through a small grove of cottonwood and elm near the base of a hill of yellowish clay. I could smell the smoke of wood-fires. Suddenly Pinkney put a hand on my arm, then pointed, and through the leaves we could see the tents, at least a dozen of them, with a few buffalo-hide lodges scattered here and there. Yet it was obvious enough from the size of the fires. This was a white man's camp, although Indians might be present.

I wiped my palms on my pants. My mouth felt suddenly dry. There must be between fifty and a hundred men down there. Against the sky I could see smoke rising from the steamboat.

It was slow going through the brush, yet all of us were accustomed to travel in the wilds and we moved in single file, skirting the camp.

Along the shore there were willows. We moved in among them and when I edged forward, she was there, the huge head leaning above me, jaws open, eyes distended. Shocked, I drew back as if fearing to be seen.

I was afraid to hesitate; a slight haze of smoke and steam marked the sky. If we waited her fires might go out and her boilers grow cold. If that happened there would be no chance, it could take half a day to fire a cold engine.

Stepping into the water, I led the way to the side of the hull, catching hold of the rail, I swung aboard. All was still. Somewhere aft I could hear a murmur of voices. One by one the others slipped aboard.

"Let slip those lines," I whispered. "With luck she'll drift away from camp. Do any of you know how to tell if she's running enough steam pressure? I've some sense of her workings but I'm not an engineer."

"Aye." McQuarrie bobbed his head. "I can give the mechanics a try if I have to."

"Well, reverse her back into the current and work with Jambe to bring a gun or two to bear on that camp. LeBrun, you take the helm and Pinkney will try and watch your backs. I'm going to make a quick search of the ship and see how many are still aboard." I handed the Pauly and it's cartridge pouch to Pinkney who had proven to be the best shot out of our group.

I clapped him on the shoulder and started aft. Inching down the deck I could hear voices and saw light through an open port in one of the cabin doors. Pausing, I listened. Tabitha was speaking. "Of course not. Captain Macklem, what you suggest is impossible, and what you plan is absurd."

"Absurd, is it?" I could sense under the casualness, a tension. She had a way of testing a man and it sounded like he had fallen for it just as I once had. "We know what we are doing, Tabitha, our plans are made. Even as we speak some of them are encamped near Fort Atkinson, on the Missouri, others are near St. Louis.

"My men are in Natchez, in New Orleans, and are ready to move against Fort Armstrong as soon as I gather my men and move down river. Prior to that certain officials in New Orleans, Natchez and St. Louis will be killed . . . in one way or another. With resistance paralyzed and communications cut off, we shall be in complete control. Once in control additional forces, European forces, will move up from the Gulf to join us."

"Captain, or Colonel, or whatever you now call yourself," Tabitha's tone was cool, confident. "You still have time to bring this farce to an end and get out of this without being tried for treason. You have been so sure you were moving in secrecy that you never realized how obvious you had become."

"Obvious?"

"Of course. My office had reports from New Orleans as early as 1818 that something was in the wind. We knew of Torville's connection by the following year. My father's correspondents kept him advised of your efforts to recruit men in Mexico as well as in New Orleans, and my father informed the general commanding the western districts.

"When you re-entered the country from Quebec and murdered that poor Captain Foulsham, Talon reported his murder to the government. He did not say as much but I believe he was quite sure who had done it."

"Yes," Macklem admitted, "that was a mistake, I should have killed him at once."

"You tried, didn't you? I heard about that."

A chair creaked as somebody sat up. "You mean he knew it was me?"

"Of course. You really haven't fooled anyone . . . not for a minute. Had you put the whole show upon the stage of the biggest theatre in New York or Paris you could not have had a more knowing audience."

"You talk very well, Tabitha," he was trying to maintain his calm, "but even if what you say is true, I still have you, I have Mrs. Higgs and I have Charles."

She was silent for a moment, during which time I marveled at her self-possession. "Yes, you do and, at the moment, you can do with us as you wish. But that doesn't make your plans any less short-sighted. How many of those men out there will remain loyal when they realize you cannot succeed?"

Under my feet I felt the desk tilt ever so slightly. The boat was adrift. Surely, Macklem would notice it, but he was seated, so perhaps less aware. I could hear a muffled clang and the sound of movement aft. I nervously looked into the dark, but then relaxed slightly, the soft hush of steam from the boilers had picked up . . . McQuarrie was at work.

"To be guilty of such a plot as this," Tabitha said, "a man must be both a great egotist as well as an optimist. He must believe himself vastly more intelligent than anyone else, and he must also believe all his plans will turn out right. My father would have never put money in such an operation as this, Captain. It has too many loop-holes. You must want, very desperately, to believe in it."

"One need not be that intelligent to out-wit a pack of fools," Macklem growled. "And, those who are not fools are asleep. This land lies ready for the taking."

She smiled. "Every crack-pot adventurer in the western hemisphere has believed that. Citizen Genet tried it in 1793, and Aaron Burr had some such plan. As for Wilkinson, he was always plotting. One of this spies, Philip Nolan, was hung as an illegal horse-trader. In Texas, wasn't it?"

"Within two months, this territory will be mine," he sneered. Nevertheless, I believed her talk was reaching him. For some reason, perhaps simply that she was a beautiful woman, he needed her to believe it.

"No. Within a few weeks you will be hanged," she replied.

He got to his feet. "You are very sure of yourself, Tabitha," he said gently, "all of which makes bringing you to your knees more enjoyable." He turned toward the door, and I drew back. Then he asked, "Tabitha, do you know where Charles is now?"

"Charles?" She turned sharply toward him, and he laughed.

"Amusing how tender a woman can feel about her

brother. If you wish to know, we've decided to use Charles as an example for you. We—"

Suddenly, he felt the movement in the deck, and lunged for the door. At the same instant there was a yell of alarm from aft, then a shot followed by the rush of feet and the sound of clashing arms.

As Macklem reached the door to the deck, I stepped into it.

He reacted instantaneously and struck out hard and I took the punch coming in. It struck with numbing force, and we both staggered back into the cabin. His left fist caught me over the eye with a blow like a club. He threw a high right that I instinctively ducked, hitting him under the heart. Piling in close, I smashed away with both fists at his body, but was shoved off and hit again over the eye. I felt a trickle of blood from a cut, slipped inside his next punch and slammed two more to the wind.

His body was like iron, and he neatly turned aside, throwing me off-balance. Before I could turn, he hit me just below the ear but I took the punch standing and turned on him. I think he was in shock! He had expected me to fall, instead, I looked at him and laughed.

I was hurt. I was badly shaken and if he had known how badly he'd have killed me. We came together then, punching with both hands and every blow he struck shook me to my heels.

He jerked his knee toward my crotch, but I brought my own knee up across my other leg to block it. He shook me with a right to the head and stepped in, his left fingers clawing for my eyes. I sank my face against his shoulder and ripped short, brutal punches to his wind.

He shoved me off then, and for an instant we faced each other.

"You can fight," he said, contemptuously. "You can fight just a little. Now I am going to kill you!"

He came in fast and I threw a punch at his face. He went under it and grabbed my left leg, lifting it high as he jammed his palm against my face. As he did so he slid his leg behind mine and I went backward over it to the floor. My pistols jolted from my sash, clattering to the deck. He followed up immediately, moving toward the guns but he had not figured on my coming up so fast. I had hit the deck hard, but hit it rolling and was on my feet moving into him.

The steamboat gave a lurch as it hit the current and McQuarrie engaged the engine. The great paddle wheel dug in pulling the dragon boat back from the shore.

Macklem slipped on the rolling deck and I caught his left arm in a hammer-lock, pushing it toward his shoulder. He turned throwing his right across my two arms locking them behind his back, then he threw me over his leg to the deck.

This time I was slower getting up and he caught me in the wind with a vicious kick. I felt a stab of pain and gasped for breath going to my knees. He tried to step back to get distance but I threw myself forward, grabbing his legs.

He smashed his knee against the side of my face and knocked me sprawling under a table. He kicked me twice before I could get out, the second kick on the side of the neck and shoulder as I was coming up.

My right caught him on the chin, a short, wicked hook from close in, and it shook him. He stepped back, measured me with a left, missed a right as I came in close, and he tried to rabbit-punch me behind the neck. Strong as he was, I began to realize I was stronger still and bulled him back against the bulkhead where I hit him twice in the body.

Suddenly there was a terrific concussion from the deck as a gun was fired, then a second and a third. From ashore there were wild yells . . . then a fourth shot.

My face was numb and there was blood running into my eyes. His own face was smooth and hard, unblemished, yet I noted there was no longer the supreme self-confidence now, I had him fighting for his life . . . but so was I. Tabitha had tried to skirt past him but he blocked her, possibly afraid she might reach my pistols or perhaps out of a simple animal instinct to control her, even now.

We sparred a moment. He jabbed at my face, and I went under it. He had kind of half-stepped back and was waiting with his right cocked for me to come in. Instead, I feinted, then smashed him on the chin with a right. His eyes blinked, and I hit him again.

Now he circled warily. For the first time I believe he realized he might not win. In the narrow confines of the cabin, we moved toward each other. Tabitha had drawn back into a corner, wide-eyed. She was skirting around toward where my pistols lay but again he blocked her, shoving her deeper into the compartment and knocking her into the bunk.

There was a pound of rushing feet on the deck outside and above, a scream, a splash, and then a cannon roared again. By the feel of the boat we were well into the current now. Suddenly, he half-crouched and his hand went to his boot and came up with a knife. "Sorry!" he said.

"But I've business aloft!" He lunged with the blade, not slashing as he might have, but thrusting like a swordsman.

Slapping the knife-hand with my left to push it out of line with my body, I grabbed his wrist with my right and stepping across in front of him, spilled him to the deck. A sudden lurch of the vessel as it hit rock or a snag in the dark river threw me, and I fell to the deck facing him.

My two pistols were there. He grabbed for one, I for the other. I pawed the hammer back and we both fired!

I felt a sudden burn as from a red-hot iron across my shoulder, and he was staring at me, his mouth open and his lower jaw shattered. Blood was soaking his shirt as he peered at the gun, aware that it had the capacity to fire again but unknowing of its mechanism.

I showed him. Grasping the cylinder in my left hand, I pushed the gun forward with my right. I rotated the mechanism, a new chamber snapping into place, and then, as I pulled my hand away, I palmed back the hammer. His eyes met mine, the mystery solved, but then I fired into him again, and he slumped on the deck and he died. I got slowly to my feet then staggered and fell back against the bulkhead.

Somebody loomed into the doorway and I turned, half-blind with blood and sweat. I started to pull the cylinder back to rotate it again.

"Don't shoot!" It was Jambe-de-Bois. "It's all right. It's all over!"

Backing up I fell against the bunk, gasping for breath as though I'd never get enough into my lungs, I tilted my head back against the bulkhead.

McQuarrie came over and began to wipe the blood

from my face. "We found Charlie. Butlin got him loose and brought him to us. Then we opened fire on their camp. We shot into their camp-fires. It scattered them. Mrs. Higgs was locked in the cabin next door."

"Is anybody hurt?"

"A few scratches. They tried to come aboard from a boat after we were in the stream. We hit something and it damaged the paddle wheel but we can still move. We were lucky, I guess."

"Torville is dead," Macaire was saying, and there was a lot of confused talk.

Tabitha was standing against the wall, only now she was trembling.

"You'd better sit down," I suggested, and she crossed over and sat down beside me. Something was bothering me, a riddle that in my exhaustion and pain seemed to have solved itself.

"Macklem was Torville?" I asked, and she nodded.

Jambe-de-Bois came into the cabin again, "Where to?"

"Pittsburgh," I said, "I've got a boat to build." I looked around at Tabitha. "Want to come along?"

"Yes," she said, "I've never built a boat."

POSTSCRIPT

By Beau L'Amour

THE MID-1970s were a very productive and very turbulent time for my father. His newest releases were selling more and more copies; but while these numbers were improving, they were still relatively modest. What surprised everyone was how well the old titles, what is called the "back list," was doing. To this day Louis L'Amour has never had a title go out of print, a situation almost unknown for a writer with so many books to his name.

The expanding sales of all of his titles enabled our family to move to a new and better neighborhood. Eventually, it allowed an extensive addition to be built onto the new house, and it gave Dad the confidence to make another attempt to change the direction of his career.

Throughout the *Lost Treasures* series, I have documented my father's attempts to avoid being trapped in just one genre. After an early string of successful western novels in the 1950s, he had attempted to broaden his resume by adding historical novels like *The Walking Drum*, nonfiction books, and the sort of exotic adventure stories that brought him success in the days of the pulp magazines. When publishers failed to respond to these ideas, he eventually created a plan to gradually expand the boundaries of the westerns he was writing to include different time periods, locales, and subject matter, breaking away from what was traditionally expected. This was all decades before the current era of mixing genres began. In the mid twentieth century, stretching the accepted limitations, particularly with a western, was considered fairly controversial.

In 1973 Dad published *The Ferguson Rifle,* a "frontier" novel set not too long after the Revolutionary War. In 1974 he came out with both *The Californios,* a story that played out in the Mexican California of the 1840s and contained elements of science fiction, and *Sackett's Land,* a story that mostly took place in Elizabethan England.

Rivers West, which arrived in 1975, was clearly inspired by a number of historical attempts to seize the territory that eventually became the Louisiana Purchase. The best known of these plots was a conspiracy masterminded by Aaron Burr, once the vice president of the United States. The goal seems to have been to create a breakaway nation in the western lands. While the exact outlines of that plan are still debated today, Burr was ultimately charged with treason. It is quite likely that this event helped motivate the more practical aspects of America's "Manifest Destiny": As long as the United States was uncertain who its neighbor to the west was going to be, it would remain in an uncomfortable strategic dilemma. How to control the territory from the Mississippi "border states" to the Pacific was the nation's most significant geopolitical security challenge for much of the nineteenth century.

Set in the early 1820s, *Rivers West* was not only a gentle step toward opening the minds of my father's audience and his publisher to stories beyond the typical cattle drives and town marshals, but he also hoped it would be a step toward greater credibility in general. Dad used to joke that if a book was written about the time before the Civil War and the country east of the Mississippi, it was likely to be seen as a "historical novel" rather than a lowly "western." *Rivers West* was an attempt to play in that eastern arena of the early frontier.

It was the third Louis L'Amour book to be published in hardcover under a new deal between Bantam and the Saturday Review Press. Besides being a tentative exploration of the hardcover market, this was also an attempt to get Dad's work reviewed by some of the major news outlets. Because of the sheer volume of novels being published as paperback originals, and a certain amount of snobbery, the critics rarely paid attention to any books other than hardcover. While my father had initially seen releasing in hardback as an unnecessary complication, by the 1970s it became a significant step toward taking his work to a wider audience.

Dad's approach to writing was all about productivity. He tried to finish three novels a year and, as is obvious from the contents of *Louis L'Amour's Lost Treasures Volumes 1* and 2, he started many more than that. These work habits stemmed from a couple of different sources. First among them was a concern about money. The sale of an individual copy brought in only a few cents. A number of writers in that era did quite well, but most of these were workhorses like my dad, men and women who had a lot of ideas and could churn out the pages at a prodigious rate.

Many people think of my father as being staggeringly successful but, in the 1970s, that period of his life was only just beginning. By then he was already well into his sixties and had no idea when his work might drop from popularity, or how long he would live. For these reasons, and because he had a great number of stories he wanted to complete before his time on earth was over, he was highly motivated. As any L'Amour fan knows, his death left many projects incomplete. Dad's writing, to a great extent, was a race against time.

So, all my father really wanted to do was work. More specifically, he just wanted to write *new* stories. Once he had figured out how a plot was going to pay off and he had typed the last page, his interest in any particular tale was pretty much over.

In most cases Dad's manuscripts needed very little editing to make them ready for publication. However, beginning with *Rivers West,* Dad expressed some irritation about the liberties editors were taking with his work. This situation came to a head a year and a half later when Dad discovered at the last minute that the manuscript of *To the Far Blue Mountains* had been drastically cut. Setting aside his normally easygoing attitude, he demanded that the copies being delivered to the wholesalers be recalled. A more complete version was quickly printed and sent out to replace them.

You might think that such a drastic remedy would have created a long-term solution, but a similar problem was allowed to occur with *Fair Blows the Wind,* and that time Dad truly boiled over. He sent a long and angry letter to Marc Jaffe, the editorial director of Bantam Books, expressing exactly what he objected to in exhaustive detail. In response, *Fair Blows the Wind* was re-edited and a number of important changes were made regarding how the L'Amour brand was handled. I suspect that these problems stemmed from the hardcover publishers, but since Dad's overall deal was with Bantam, they were required to sort the situation out. I have quoted Dad's letter to Marc Jaffe at length in the *Lost Treasures* postscript to *Fair Blows the Wind*, but for our purposes here this is the important passage:

> . . . RIVERS WEST, because of what was done to it, is one of my least satisfactory books. I would have to check the mss. but my guess is that at least 100 pages were cut out of it.

When I read that I knew that I was going to have to make a "restored" edition of *Rivers West* a part of the *Louis L'Amour's Lost Treasures* series. If a hundred pages had actually been cut out of the book, they simply had to be replaced and the book re-edited. However, what had happened to this story, and what I would be able to do about it, ended up being a much more complicated situation.

Our manuscripts are kept in a series of fireproof file cabinets in a long narrow room that is reserved for archiving our many projects. The space is crowded with all sorts of objects: canisters of movie film, boxes of old promotional materials, scrapbooks, and cases full of tape recordings. Searching through these records showed that the original manuscript pages had indeed been returned to us. And, as I expected, the *Rivers West* pages showed signs of hard use. Notes and editor's marks were scribbled everywhere. In places the paper was torn or crumpled, and sections were even missing.

The first thing I did was to try and compare that manuscript to a current copy of the paperback. Very quickly I realized that many of the editorial changes indicated on the original typewritten pages were not reflected in the paperback copy. Amidst the scrawls in several different handwriting styles, someone had written "stet," a publishing term for "let it stand," alongside a number of sections that had been marked for deletion. Clearly, there had been a second or even third pass at some later point in time, and material that had once been marked for removal had been put back in.

Was this evidence that someone had responded to an objection of my father's? Had some changes been reversed before publication of the hardcover, or was it an indication that the paperback edition, published a year later, was a bit more complete? I have no idea. It might even be possible that certain pieces of text were put back in a few years after the letter to Marc Jaffe quoted above. Neither I nor anyone I could get in touch with remembers exactly what happened.

What is true is this: While many changes had been made, I was certain that a hundred pages had *not* been cut out of it. In total I doubt that more than twenty pages had been removed. I'm guessing that by the time Dad wrote to Marc in 1977, irritation over several cases of excessive editing had made the memory of the changes to *Rivers West* feel more dramatic than they really were.

Carefully going over the manuscript, and comparing it with other work of my father's, I realized what had caused this particular novel to receive additional attention. Frankly, in its original form, it was a mess.

Typically, Dad would produce drafts that, while they might contain a few errors, were internally quite consistent. In the case of *Rivers West*, there were shifts between first and third person, a good deal of repetition, some unnecessary digressions, and confusion about the exact location of certain parts of the action. The manuscript showed signs of distraction, possibly even some sort of emotional upheaval. Given its release in the spring of 1975, the most likely time for the book to have been written is early to mid-'74. While I can't think of, nor find reference to, any particular short-term event in my father's life that might explain these problems, it's my guess that some of the writing was done a bit earlier and that what disturbed Dad's ability to concentrate was our move from the house we owned in West Hollywood to our new home in West Los Angeles in the summer of 1973.

Of course, it wasn't just moving. And the disruption wasn't limited to just that one year. First there had been a good deal of house hunting. Mom did most of that, but Dad became involved every time it seemed like she had found the right sort of place. To make matters worse, they were committed to closing a deal while school was out. I was about to begin junior high and, given the way the public school districts were set up, if we didn't lock down an address in West L.A., I would be forced to attend a junior high in a much tougher part of town that was many miles away and in the wrong direction. Looking back on the time period of the 1970s I have to say that I'm very grateful for their decision!

Once we did find a house, there was all the expected packing and moving and unpacking. Somehow my mother pulled this off and still got us all to Durango, Colorado, for a few weeks' vacation at the Strater Hotel before we had to move in. As I remember it, my mother, father, and sister went straight to the new house from the airport and lived out of their suitcases until the storage company delivered all our stuff. My memory is a bit foggy because I took the opportunity to spend a few days with a family friend who lived about an hour away.

The biggest problem with our new home was that there was no good place for Dad to write except for a spot right in the center of all the chaos. For three years or so he worked on a plywood table loaned to him by one of the carpenters who had been helping to renovate parts of the house. He had no privacy and was surrounded by boxes of books and piles of papers. Some had probably been packed with an eye to what he thought he would need until we got organized. But I'm guessing that didn't work out all that well. A frequent memory from those years was of him going through piles of boxes in other rooms, patiently searching for a book or a manuscript or something of the sort.

If that wasn't enough, not long before we moved in, just before we went to Colorado, Mom discovered that under the linoleum tiles in the main hall and dining room and under the carpet on the stairs were beautiful Spanish tile and hardwood floors dating back to the house's construction in the 1920s. I fear we all went a bit crazy pulling up garish early-1960s floor coverings to see what wonders lurked beneath. This made a complete mess of the area around Dad's desk and required various floor finishers and painters to come in and sort things out.

And there was also all the drama associated with both my sister and me starting new schools, trying to fit into a new neighborhood, and our dog constantly running away. It was a chaotic time in our lives—ultimately good in every way, but full of confusion and difficulty.

REGARDLESS OF WHAT caused the rough condition of *Rivers West*, I decided that my job was to try to incorporate as much of Dad's original manuscript as I could into a new *Lost Treasures* edition. At the same time, I needed to make it read as swiftly and clearly as any other Louis L'Amour novel written in that era. The missing pieces were not all that significant, the longest being no more than two to three pages and the majority just a paragraph, sentence, or even a few words. I don't believe the changes I've made have transformed the book into a lost masterpiece. For the most part, I doubt readers will even notice.

Thanks to our attorney and his optical character recognition software, I got all of the original text scanned and in place. Then I started my own edit, cleaning up the inconsistencies and digressions that plagued the original manuscript. That meant some cutting—when a problem needs to be solved, my first choice is always to cut rather than to add material; occasionally, I deleted elements that had been removed by earlier editors. But it also meant expanding certain ideas. There were passages that, rather than being cut, could be made to function better within the framework of the story. This is the significant advantage I have over a normal editor: I know my father's life, his work, and his varied interests well enough to add material here and there in a manner that has a close relationship to the way he thought.

For example, Dad took a lot of pride in the accuracy of his landscapes. Yet in the last few chapters of *Rivers West,* his characters sometimes seemed to be close to the juncture between the Missouri and Mississippi rivers and at other times quite a ways up the Missouri near its intersection with the Kansas River. This was probably the best evidence that there was turmoil in Dad's life during the writing of this novel.

The earlier editors had struggled to straighten all of this out but hadn't done as clean a job of it as I would have liked. I fixed the situation by putting some of the original material back in while doing some cutting and filling so it all made a bit more sense. I suspect that Dad toyed with the idea of having the steamboat *Western Engineer* bombard a town or fort near the Missouri's juncture with the Mississippi. If so, he probably scrapped this dramatic scene, and then redirected his action up the Missouri, because such a significant event was not something that actually existed in the historical record.

I also took the opportunity to play up certain elements to make more sense of Dad's having chosen to include them in the first place. One such case is my adding a few specifics about the use of the Collier pistols in the final fight with Macklem. Dad liked to throw in interesting historical details, like arming a character with such advanced technology as the Collier revolver and Pauly pinfire rifle. In *Rivers West,* possibly because my father had initially planned, or was hoping to write, a longer book, the inclusion of these inventions came too late in the narrative to play any sort of special role.

Thanks to information from the wonderful "Forgotten Weapons" YouTube videos, I was able to pay off the idea of Dad's having included these innovative firearms. After seeing a Collier up close and hearing a discussion of how it functioned, I added the moment where Macklem realizes the pistol has the potential for another shot but doesn't know how to operate its mechanism. It was also a subtly ironic way of reinforcing the point that my father was making earlier in the narrative about Macklem's, or Torville's, being a retrograde figure out of step with the times.

It is not always the case that artists perfectly understand their own work. You can tell from Dad's letter saying he thought more than a hundred pages had been cut that he imagined *Rivers West* to be a bigger, longer novel than it actually was. It seems clear that if Dad had spent more time analyzing and polishing his story, he would have realized he had not achieved his goals and that *Rivers West* required another draft. On the other hand, rehashing too many details would have reduced his output, caused him to run the risk of writer's block, and made him considerably less happy with the overall process. If there is one fundamental quality in any Louis L'Amour novel, it is the fact that the reader can sense the joyous energy he brought to the act of writing. Finding a balance between writing new material and perfecting that which is already written is always difficult. I fear that all creation is full of such trade-offs.

THERE IS ONE last aspect to the story of *Rivers West* and the character of Jean Talon to present here. Dad made a few notes on a sequel:

> Talon is approached by a man in a saloon. Very secret. Handle it with much suspense like a modern day spy story. He could repair a steamboat? Fix it up?
>
> There is a secret cache of furs. A quick trip up river,and a quick trip down, and furs enough to make them all rich, for the moment. [They had been] Abandoned [when a Sioux raiding party] came, but hidden, well-hidden.
>
> They would need a crew. He has Jambe de Bois with him, but the others are a rough lot. The place to which they will go is far up the river, they must hide the boat, go overland. When they come back they'll be on the run, and then down the river fast.
>
> Why so much secrecy? Army doesn't want to stir up the Indians?
>
> Very secret trip into unknown country travel by night, hidden by day when possible. Talon distrusts crew, distrusts leader of the venture. There are three other men he has hired, one is mysteriously

lost overboard. He takes on a lone man at a wood-lot who knows something about leader, but is very cautious, not sure if he can trust Talon.

Perhaps leader had gone in with a party of trappers and returned alone? Perhaps he had come upon some of the party murdered . . . not by Indians. Cache is worth thousands. Trade with Indians, loot from Indians, trapping by themselves.

Dealings with Indians, some folklore, much background, color, atmosphere, solid western material.

Menace from inside, from outside, haunting nights, talks with leader who may be a bit off-course, but a dangerous man. But an intelligent man, not wise, but bright.

Ultimately, I believe the reason Dad did not pursue this and any number of the other Sackett, Chantry, and Talon story ideas he occasionally jotted down was that he eventually got a structure for the overall series set in his mind. Rather than just writing random adventures, he wanted to fill in the timeline from the seventeenth to the end of the nineteenth century with stories that were essential rather than merely additional. That meant focusing his planning on novels about a Sackett and a Chantry during the Revolutionary War, a Chantry in Mexican- or Spanish-era Santa Fe, and something to do with railroading or the era of the great surveyors that occurred just before the Civil War.

Once he closed up the gaps in the series I'm not sure if he intended to simply move on to do other things or if historical events like the Spanish-American War would have drawn his favorite characters away from the American frontier and into the Caribbean and the Philippines. Even World War I might have played a role in his "three family" series. Personally, I think that returning to early-twentieth-century Europe would have been the perfect bookend to the stories of the early Sacketts, Chantrys, and Talons arriving on the American frontier from their homes in England and France. And writing stories set in Cuba and the Philippines certainly would have allowed him to circle back to creating the sort of exotic adventure stories that he had so enjoyed writing early on in his career.

BEAU L'AMOUR
SEPTEMBER 2025

ABOUT LOUIS L'AMOUR

"I think of myself in the oral tradition—
as a troubadour, a village taleteller, the man
in the shadows of the campfire. That's the way
I'd like to be remembered—as a storyteller.
A good storyteller."

IT IS DOUBTFUL that any author could be as at home in the world re-created in his novels as Louis Dearborn L'Amour. Not only could he physically fill the boots of the rugged characters he wrote about, but he literally "walked the land my characters walk." His personal experiences as well as his lifelong devotion to historical research combined to give Mr. L'Amour the unique knowledge and understanding of people, events, and the challenge of the American frontier that became the hallmarks of his popularity.

As a boy growing up in Jamestown, North Dakota, he absorbed all he could about his family's frontier heritage, including the story of his great-grandfather who was scalped by Sioux warriors.

Spurred by an eager curiosity and a desire to broaden his horizons, Mr. L'Amour left home at the age of fifteen and enjoyed a wide variety of jobs, including seaman, lumberjack, elephant handler, skinner of dead cattle, miner, and officer in the Transportation Corps during World War II. He was a voracious reader and collector of books. His personal library contained 17,000 volumes.

Mr. L'Amour "wanted to write almost from the time I could talk." After developing a widespread following for the many frontier and adventure stories he wrote for fiction magazines, Mr. L'Amour published his first full-length novel, *Hondo,* in the United States in 1953. Every one of his more than 120 books is in print; there are more than 300 million copies of his books in print worldwide, making him one of the bestselling authors in modern literary history. His books have been translated into twenty languages, and more than forty-five of his novels and stories have been made into feature films and television movies.

His hardcover bestsellers include *The Lonesome Gods, The Walking Drum* (his twelfth-century historical novel), *Jubal Sackett, Last of the Breed,* and *The Haunted Mesa.* His memoir, *Education of a Wandering Man,* was a leading bestseller in 1989. Audio dramatizations and adaptations of many L'Amour stories are available from Random House Audio.

The recipient of many great honors and awards, in 1983 Mr. L'Amour became the first novelist ever to be awarded the Congressional Gold Medal by the United States Congress in honor of his life's work. In 1984 he was also awarded the Medal of Freedom by President Reagan.

Louis L'Amour died on June 10, 1988. His wife, Kathy, and their two children, Beau and Angelique, carry the L'Amour publishing tradition forward.